DOREEN KERRY

An imaginary quest for justice in the
aftermath of a terrible loss

DOREEN KERRY

# When Angels Fall

An imaginary quest for justice in the
aftermath of a terrible loss

**MEREO**
Cirencester

# Mereo Books

1A The Wool Market Dyer Street Cirencester Gloucestershire GL7 2PR
An imprint of Memoirs Publishing www.mereobooks.com

When Angels Fall: 978-1-86151-888-0

First published in Great Britain in 2017
by Mereo Books, an imprint of Memoirs Publishing

The address for Memoirs Publishing Group Limited can be found at
www.memoirspublishing.com

The Memoirs Publishing Group Ltd Reg. No. 7834348

The Memoirs Publishing Group supports both The Forest Stewardship Council® (FSC®) and the PEFC® leading international forest-certification organisations. Our books carrying both the FSC label and the PEFC® and are printed on FSC®-certified paper. FSC® is the only forest-certification scheme supported by the leading environmental organisations including Greenpeace. Our paper procurement policy can be found at www.memoirspublishing.com/environment

Typeset in 12/18pt Century Schoolbook
by Wiltshire Associates Publisher Services Ltd. Printed and bound in Great Britain
by Printondemand-Worldwide, Peterborough PE2 6XD

# PREFACE

Imagine looking forward to that special breakfast in which you insist on having your eggs sunny side up. At the cooking stage everything needs to be done just right, or the whites will be underdone or the yolks overcooked. What a disappointment that would be.

Imagine then, that you are looking forward to celebrating your Ruby Wedding anniversary with the one and only love of your life, and suddenly things go horribly wrong. That's a little different. You may be able to revive those eggs, salvage them even, but if not, there is still the chance for you to start all over again. The same cannot be said when medical care goes horribly wrong, depriving you forever of the most important person in your life, and all you are left with is a bad taste in your mouth.

It is said that widowhood can open new doors that you may not have chosen to open, but which you need to go through in order to survive the years ahead. I hate exercise, fly fishing is not for me and I am not prepared to put myself through owning, loving and losing a third pet. I may fall in love again, but I have no plans for the next fifty years or so, which leaves only my writing to keep me sane.

I have found in me an inner strength which enables me to vent my feelings of anger and sadness in a cutting but light-hearted way, yet constructive from the point of view of a nurse where there is a fine line between a medical mishap and sheer negligence.

I know a click of my ruby house slippers will not send me to Kansas, but I just cannot tear myself away from the yellow brick road which promises to lead to justice. However, I could do with a little help along the way.

Join me in my 'pop up' courtroom, where a Lurex-festooned judge sits in judgement on those who deprived hubby and me of our special anniversary and all the anniversaries to follow, and indulge in a game of 'spot the indifference.' I am not here to depress, I am here to entertain, though in a most poignant way. Intrigued? Then pop this book in your shopping trolley right now, and make me and my publisher happy.

Doreen Kerry
March 2018

# CONTENTS

# THE NEW RECRUIT

———◦⊰⊱◦———

In my previous literary 'voyage' you would have come to know me as 'Camomile', Jerry (aka Paul Henried)'s love interest, who I had met on a cruise ship in an altered ego state. As the white cliffs of Dover were upon me I disembarked and it was the parting of the waves for us when he did an 'about turn' back to Boston (*Now Voyager,* 1942). I told him it would be quicker by Hovercraft, but he was fearful that he might not be able to smoke on board.

Not only had I spent weeks working long and hard after landing the part of Scarlett O'Hara (*Gone With the Wind,* 1939) and even longer at trying to perfect a southern accent (and I do not mean a Somerset one), after the director's agent had bypassed almost 2000 young women before he took me on, I also had to contend with Clark Gable's bad breath during our kissing scenes. Mr Selznick had conveniently forgotten to tell me that my co-star had false teeth, so maybe that is why the other potential actresses who did get auditioned had decided not to give it their best shot!

Poor guy, it seems he had been wearing them since he was eighteen years old, but they fitted well; tailor-made for him, you might say, just as the part of Rhett Butler was.

Equally crazy, one would have witnessed my mad-hatter antics as I fictionally travelled through the different times in my life in a souped-up version of H G Well's Time Machine, the storyline inspired by my love of the iconic Hollywood movie 'prop.' In that I took my readers through the realms of comparison and contrast as in a cruise ship versus a hospital ward, stateroom attendants versus nursing and medical personnel, and a package holiday versus a hospital admission.

As I tip-toed in and out of time and in true TV and movie fashion retained my right to remain silent lest anything I did say might have been misquoted and used against my publisher, my readers were able to witness an interplay between events in my life and the behaviour of some of the characters that crossed my path.

I am not the Jabberwocky. My neck may be a little scrawny, but that's only age-related. I am nowhere near twelve feet tall and I have neither 'jaws that bite nor claws that catch' so do not slay – or should I say, slate me (*Alice through the Looking Glass,* 1871).

I am more like the gentle Alice who has tried to apply rational understanding over completely irrational arguments under very trying circumstances in trying to seek justice for the loss of my husband after so many years. I now have a very tall top hat with a silk ribbon around it and a 60¾ label sticking out from it. What could possibly have been the inspiration for that, I wonder?

Just as the old films sought to have cliffhangers to tease audiences back, it was my intention then that my readers should return to see whether or not I had actually put the brake on things since my last musings or whether I still aspired to find the truth, no matter how long it took. I have to say that I gave wholeheartedly in to the latter.

The events of several Christmases past have seen me, an ordinarily timid woman, come to life in a world that I never knew existed when I went looking for answers outside my own backyard and encountered a hospital complaint system that was set to test my patience beyond all reasonable doubt after the only man I have ever loved came to a sticky end barely six days into his admission.

Many have ruffled my feathers over the years, but a scared 'crow' I am no longer. Whilst I may not have interchangeable heads that resemble a turnip, mangelwurzel or swede, I have had to wear many different hats during that time to suit my particular field of expertise in each of the different scenarios (*Worzel Gummidge,* (ITV, 1979-1981).

My sense of humour was not designed then to demean or disparage the medical profession, any more than it sets out to do now, but I hope I can hit home real issues through an equally captivating story and even more memorable characters, and whilst my story has a high degree of realism it is intended that my audience should interpret it from my unique viewpoint as uncovered in a highly incredible environment.

'Camomile' may be long gone, but as I continue my venture of principality this Wednesday morning over a cup of tea, I will I take a minute to introduce my new altered ego state – someone who has appropriately 'evolved' in a desperate attempt to try to get to the bottom of things once and for all.

My name is Brooke – Brooke Bond – quite apt don't you think as a tea connoisseur? Since it would be wrong of me to assume that all my readers are in their twilight years I should explain that once upon a time there was a man called Arthur Brooke and in the late 19th century he decided to market his own brand of tea. In this day and age marketers pitch for recognition of their products in some weird and wonderful ways, but Arthur had come up with a very clever way of getting customers to buy his.

As a child I did not really go a bundle on cereals, but I did acquire a taste for Rice Krispies, which was partly due to the fact that there was always a 'secret' toy hidden among the aerated pebbled grains, and I wanted to snap, crackle and pop my way towards collecting all that was on offer.

Why Rice Krispies of all things, you might say? Well, perhaps it was the fact that Mum's maiden name was Rice. As Mum and Dad's first child I amusingly liked to consider myself to be the first 'Ricicle' out of the box, if that does not sound too crude, although she had assumed her married name by that time, yet I was not a secret love child nor just something to be played with.

The point is, I do not think I would have bonded with the cereal had it not been for the charm-like 'giveaways,' and likewise, Arthur had established his own way of bonding with children through their mothers by introducing free educational tea cards into the packets of leafy tea, and voilà – everyone was a winner! And that, in a nutshell, is how the name Brooke Bond evidently came about.

So I have now assumed the role of a lonely widow detective inspired by my own collection of tea cards, as I continue my quest into what happened to hubby T, during which you will get a glimpse into the justice system and how the law works, in my estimation. Much as I like the idea of being able to tell my story through the use of pictorial cards, it would be quite impractical, and besides they would most definitely top the 50 mark!

If I were to say to you 'B52' you might consider me to be very hip-hop, but rest assured I am not talking about any American rock band, who most definitely cannot 'Give me back my Man' (B52's 1980). Nope, I am talking about B52 in the series of Arthur's card collections and specifically *The Secret Diary of Kevin Tipps* (1995) about a skateboarding and motorcycling chimp who, ironically, lived at Brooke Close with his mum and sister Samantha.

See how easily, without proper explanation, one can get the wrong end of the stick. This is the basis for my coming here today and a way to bond with my readers – especially those who have loved and lost someone very dear to them.

I grew up in a council flat in North London, as opposed to a posh one on the Kings' Road, Chelsea like James, my male spy counterpart. My trademark is my wicked sense of humour, as opposed to a Bentley (and my tea cards of course), but I have never smoked fags, whether custom made from a mix of Balkan/Turkish tobacco or any other. Should this have been the case then I would definitely have had to go one better and use hubby's Dunhill in replacement of JB's Ronson. Only the best for me!

My curiosity had me seek out a black oxidised Ronson on eBay however, just for curiosity's sake, but as yet I have been unsuccessful at locating one.

Since the start of my complaint and own investigation into hubby's death it has been a case of *Dr No* (as in 'no doctor, do not try to fob me off); I have 'Viewed the Kill' based on my own observations and if it is true as they say, that *You Only Live Twice*, then it is not right that having only had the privilege of living once, it was not for a lot longer. My films to date include *To Thatcham with Love* and *Fishfinger*, and the penny arcade on a West Country seafront had been my *Casino Royale*. Hey, when the chips are down you learn to improvise, right?

I like my sweet Martini Rossos stirred not shaken, and perhaps this week I will dine on oeufs en cocotte – that is, eggs served in a delicate way – rather than my usual style, boiled to the point of explosion. Cooking this posh variation is not the only thing where I need to get the timing right, but so too the events that are about to unfold and, in chronological order, there is no ramekin that will be big enough to accommodate what you are about to digest.

Unlike one of my more recent counterparts, have no fear that I shall be pitting my wits against a global criminal organisation or be confronting criminal leaders (2015 film). Instead you will witness an account somewhere between fact and fiction where I am pitted against a nationally recognised 'system.' I am risking it all here, and my editor is helping to break my fall, but to be honest the words 'no win, can't win' are firmly embedded in the brickwork in my backyard - so in the words of loveable singer Sam Smith (2017), 'the writing's on the wall.'

# MISS DIAGNOSIS

—◦—

'My hovercraft is full of eels.' Watch this sketch from an episode of Monty Python's Flying Circus and you cannot help but laugh at how badly the English-Hungarian phrase book has been translated. It shows the funny side of misinterpretation and the kind of bother people can get into.

Then consider the words 'missed diagnosis' and 'misdiagnosis' in the world of medicine - a non-humorous comparison – in which it this can make a huge difference when it comes to proving that unnecessary, ineffective and dangerous treatment has taken place due to diagnoses having been wrongly categorised.

I am a nurse. I spend most of my days assessing patients, as a basis for care planning. The most important thing of all is that I use a holistic approach when gathering information so that I can identify their *real* needs, from which care can be tailor-made to fit them in the same way as Clark's dentures and his acclaimed acting part. In other care settings I have found this not necessarily to be the case.

Consider for one moment, if you will, that I am the one being assessed in a hospital. I have been admitted by way of a referral letter from my GP. Unknown to me, it states that I am 'afflicted with kleptomania' – that is, a compulsion to repeatedly steal 'worthless' items – but because he is not a specialist in this kind of 'behaviour', the doc forwards me on to others who are more trained to look into the whys and wherefores of such an act.

In 'real time' I do not steal, although I have acquired over time an extensive collection of restaurant menus since hubby passed away. As a substitute for having previously sat with his father watching football one day a week when I was either belly-wobbling or secretly creating my memoirs on the laptop, our son then chose to keep up the mid-week tradition of coming round to the house, but instead of watching grown men kick a ball around a pitch he and I would go out to eat and watch as the waiters served delicious nosh onto our plates.

Before a dawn raid by the Keystone Cops seeks to recover any stolen items from my home, it should be known that permission was always granted by the restaurant owners to take the menus home. Failing that, I had no qualms in settling for their takeaway menus instead; I just wanted a souvenir, that was all, and I admit there might have been the odd 'indiscretion.'

Would this be considered 'compulsive' over 'determined'? Would a mental health assessment be in order? In such a setting, quite likely!

The assessing clinician might first wonder why this pattern of behaviour had started out so late on in my life; 'stealing' as something that teenagers or young adults might ordinarily do – a phase they might go through. Ask me and I will say: 'That's because until five years ago I rarely got to eat out at all.'

Chances are that by now, given my age, the clinicians would already be suspecting early onset of dementia. In working through their checklist I am mindful of anything else that might be misconstrued, such as:

Question: Does this woman have an alcohol problem? Is stealing a defect character that she has employed?

Ask me and I will say: So I may drink over the recommended limit of Babycham from time to time and it *is* quite possible that with one too many, I might think the sky is the limit and fail to pre-empt the shame or guilt I might feel afterwards at bringing those menus or receipts home, especially where they may have dropped into my bag accidentally.

Section 1(1) of the Theft Act 1968 provides that a

person is guilty of theft if they 'dishonestly appropriate property belonging to another with the intention of permanently depriving the other of it.'

In the first instance I could not be accused of acting dishonestly, as it would have to be proven that there was a deliberate attempt on my part to acquire it for myself, and even if the intention was then to return it to its rightful owner so that they might be deprived only temporarily, at the rate the restaurants are closing in my town the chances are they will not still be there the next time I consider returning to put things right.

Just saying!

Question: Is the urge to bring those menus home with her so powerful that she just cannot resist it?

Ask me and I will say: I can, but I don't want to.

Question: Do her actions occur spontaneously, without planning, and without any help from others?

Ask me and I will say: No, not spontaneously. I always plan to come back with a menu and there are times when my son has politely asked the owner's permission for one whilst I have been in the loo having then slipped it into my handbag (legitimately). So yes, I may have had help from 'others.'

Question: Does she take menus from public places, such as her local supermarket?

Ask me and I will say: No, I do not, as I only like to eat in secluded and select places – anywhere but on the high street.

Question: Is it because she cannot afford to buy them that she must seek to talk the owners out of giving them to her for free, as they seem pretty worthless material?

Ask me and I will say: I always say you cannot put a price on memories, so they will never be worthless to me, and yes, I can afford to pay for them if asked, although generally, given the amount our bill comes to, they should chuck one in for free in any case!

Question: Will these menus and receipts be stashed away never to be used again?

Definitely, I would say. They are stashed away in my umpteen memory books and there is no reason why they should be used anywhere after that – just some other ridiculous items that our kids would inherit from me along with those milk bottle tops that never made it onto the Blue Peter desk.

Question: Do the urges come and go or is it always there?

Ask me and I will say: The urge is always there; the urge to want to get as many as I can before I die of food poisoning.

There is the strong possibility that I would be misdiagnosed as a kleptomaniac, when all I am in fact is a woman who likes to collect menus (and meal receipts for that matter), for pleasure, not as the result of some weird obsession or to fill any 'unmet' need.

Correct Diagnosis: Collectomaniac, not Kleptomaniac.

Treatment Plan: That I don't go out any more, or take to eating out in sh***y places where the menus are not worth collecting, let alone 'stealing' in any case. Simples!

Ask anyone who knows me and they will say I also

have an 'urge' to click away with my old-fashioned camera at all family events or on holidays – even asking perfect strangers to take them for me so we can all be in the frame. Regardless of this I do not have, nor have ever had, perpetual thoughts about photography in any way, yet there is a good chance that a mental health consultant might diagnose me with an obsessive-compulsive personality disorder or deem me to have Photography Compulsive Syndrome! Perhaps the evidence base would be the stupid things I care to capture on a 35mm film roll.

Treatment Plan: Try and 'reel' it in a bit.

And what of my love for drinking tea, which might run up to six cups a day? I am not obsessed to the point where I have to work my way through all the variations other than camomile, and whilst I may be the Infection Control Link Nurse at work I do not have a whole set of tea strainers just to minimise the risk of cross-leaf contamination.

Treatment Plan: Be mindful of the diuretic effects of too much caffeine and make sure to keep a penny handy for the loo if away from home and make sure to stay slim enough to be able to get through the turnstiles.

I like to read books too. I do not have an emotional attachment to them, yet I most definitely will have for the ones that I myself get to write and have published in the future.

Treatment Plan: Buy a book on attachment theories.

Detaching away from this, I might be assessed for

my mobility status. The only mobility issue I have is being made to walk when I don't have to. As hubby used to say, 'God gave me two feet – one for the brake and one for the clutch', with which I wholeheartedly agree.

I am however, physically fit regardless. I am fully able to carry out my tasks at work with vigour and alertness (attention to the drug round) without any undue fatigue and have enough energy to respond to any emergency and then go on to enjoy my leisure time pursuits - although sitting behind my laptop on my days off might not be good for the circulation.

Treatment Plan: Cut my hours at work, put my feet up and tap away.

So who has not held a mad hatter's tea party in their garden? I have, and the plastic flamingos are still poking out from the grass as evidence of that, but I am not living on planet Zanussi, really I am not, and still the mercury poisoning has not fully taken hold since my last musings. Don't worry folks!

I have self-diagnosed that I do *not* have Mad Hatter's disease, as my hands are not trembling and I am quite capable of holding these two Babycham glasses in my hands (what I call a balanced diet) without spilling a drop. Besides, I am only practising what I preach at work – that one must aim to have between 1200 and 1500mls fluids daily.

So with no mercury coming out through my hair, eyes or fingernails, the only symptom of a personality change is that I am turning from a level-headed RGN into a crazy writer.

Treatment Plan: Warn the neighbours in advance

next time I intend to go out on the patio dressed like the White Rabbit.

So, as a crazy comparison with the real world, I could well have found my medical notes showing a *misdiagnosis* of dementia, kleptomania, OCPD, PCD, alcoholic dependency and oh, yes, mobility-wise, laziness.

As for a *missed diagnosis* then: There is the chance that the clinician might eventually read the part of the referral letter that says I have been widowed for a number of years and that all that is wrong with me is that I am suffering from grief, which was the only conclusion they needed to reach. At the very best they might consider whether or not I am suffering from Broken Heart Syndrome and carry out an X-ray which will show, by rights, that my heart is enlarged, my arteries are blocked and the blood is pumping around my body at a rate of knots. I am pretty sure I would know by now if my heart were enlarged (I have a big heart already you see), and there is nothing wrong with my arteries that cutting down on the odd bit of bacon or belly pork fat won't fix. And if my heart is enraged, then it is caused only by my anger at having to continually fight to be heard in the right places. The heart attack is on hold right now.

However, there is a good chance that none of the clinicians assigned to me would think an X-ray actually necessary, that they would seek to presume that I am clinically depressed and as a result of failing to crave the pleasurable feelings of dopamine, it is the imbalance in my brain that has made me seek comfort in my 'kleptomanic' state.

In each given scenario I might then unnecessarily end up on anti-depressant and having to live with the stigma of being classed mentally ill, resulting in being prescribed Donepezil to slow down the progression of Alzheimer's plus a daily 'dose' of the contents of a Rivastigmine transdermal patch to help enhance my memory. There is an equally good chance, therefore, that I might then end up with Lewy Body Dementia as a result of inappropriate medication, when all that's wrong with me is that I like to eat out, like to take photographs, like to drink perry juices, like to read, enjoy the tales from Wonderland and oh yes, am a grieving widow.

What I am basically trying to say in my sarcastic way is that there is an increased tendency among clinicians to medicalise patterns of behaviour and moods even if they are not that extreme yet. They fail to consider the basics whereby people can find themselves at the wrong end of a care pathway.

# MISS CONCEPTION

———◁◇▷———

A pathway to care, just so you know, is a tool that is used by healthcare professionals aimed at reducing variability in nursing and medical practice to ensure that all care provided has a proper evidence base.

In my particular role and in the particular setting in which I work, we see our clients as individuals and do not believe that the prescriptive way of gathering information is the right way to go about things. In the same way as my scatty self- assessed scenario, a person-centred approach permeates my organisation's culture of working, and hopefully the words I choose to use when writing a patient profile reflects this.

Call me a holistic model nurse if you like (don't see

many of them on the catwalk), as I like to consider the person as a whole' remembering all too well the Roper-Tierney-Logan theory (1980) from my days as a student nurse when trying to consider a client's overall journey from dependence to independence.

Should I find myself at the mercy of those who are too scared to go outside a tick box assessment, there is a real danger that I might casually be assessed as terminal, end up on a load of sedatives to keep me from shouting out 'hey you've got this all wrong' and be denied water so that my last days could be seen as being self-fulfilled. Perhaps now would be as good a time as any for me to write my own care plans on the Activities of Daily Living (or ADLs for short), should I be unfortunate to wind up in the same place hubby did all those years ago.

For the purpose of this exercise as I work through the categories one by one, I shall refer to myself as Dora (on account of how dippy I can be at times and how hubby often referred to our youngest daughter as being so even though that was not actually her name any more than it is mine).

Eating and Drinking:

Dora has a good appetite. She likes large portions of everything. She has a dislike of 'sharing platters.'

There has been *some* weight increase over the years, as she has eaten less since she was no longer cooking for two – not due to over-eating but under-eating, her body having had to compensate for that by storing fat, unaware of when she might next get a chance to eat, especially if working a 13-hour shift.

Dora does not like to be traditionally weighed monthly, as it only makes her depressed. Dora's preferred drink is Babycham, although she will settle for sweet Martini as long as it is stirred and not shaken. She tends not to exceed the recommended daily fluid intake. Dora is not alcohol dependent – let there be no misconception – and she is able to manage food and drink without any assistance.

Personal Hygiene and Grooming:

Dora is able to wash herself independently, provided the instructions on the back of the soap packet are clear, else she will work up a right old lather. If she starts frothing at the mouth, be mindful that it could be anything other than rabies.

Dora can choose her own clothing and get dressed independently, but if she inadvertently puts a jumper on inside out do not change it over, as she will consider it unlucky and associate this to with any future mishaps in her life. Other than that there are no other paranoid tendencies.

Mobility:

Dora has two working feet, as long as they are not crammed into a size 3 shoe – she wears a 4½ and requires a moderate heel. Colours to avoid: yellow and shocking pink.

When Dora walks through a storm she holds her head up high and is not afraid of the dark. At the end of the storm she believes there *is* a golden sky and the sweet silver song of a lark. Dora has walked on through every wind and has walked on through every bit of rain, even though her dreams have been tossed and blown; but she can walk on with hope in her heart as she never walks alone (thanks Jerry).

Oh, and Dora categorically states that she does not want anyone to cry for her, especially those in Argentina.

Sleeping:

Dora does not need an air mattress on her bed as her skin is intact. It may show a little age-related wear and tear, but generally it is in pretty good nick. She needs to sleep in the same double bed she has had for almost 20 years and must have two pillows at all times. Dora is looking to buy a new bed if she ever wins the postcode lottery. She has, for many years, had her eye on a lavish gold bed frame at her local Dunelm store, and even though it is only a display model, money talks, right? She only sleeps for short periods because her fictitious mind continues to work overtime.

Thinking and Deciding:

Dora is able to think for herself and make her own choices. She is very determined about what she wants and does not tolerate fools easily. Dora may resort to non-verbal gestures on occasion if she gets grossly misunderstood, using her thumb and index finger in an up and down closing movement to insinuate that the person need not keep 'going on' and that she has got their message. Dora also has a tendency to unintentionally pout.

Dora is open to criticism just so long as it is positive. She will listen but not necessarily act on the advice of others, with the exception of her editor.

Communication:

Dora claims to know three languages – English, Gibberish and Double Dutch – although English is her mother tongue. When she is having a funny five minutes she may resort to Cockney rhyming slang, but just humour her and pretend you know what the hell she is talking about.

Elimination:

Dora is fully able to take herself to the toilet – she has regular practice on account of the amount of tea she drinks – especially on Wednesdays when not at work and creating her imaginary masterpieces.

Dora does not suffer from verbal diarrhoea, unlike others she knows, and is very intolerant of people who talk out of their backsides and especially those who are inclined to pebble-dash the walls.

Breathing:

Dora says all she needs is the air that she breathes and for her readers to love her (Hollies sh**!)

Other:

Dora does not need a call bell as she can shout perfectly well; she might walk into unsafe areas, especially on the 'net' (like the time she typed in Oh Boy when trying to research an old 1960 magazine only to find herself on some dodgy male dating site).

She can regulate her own body temperature; there is always the potential for her to fall (head over heels in love with her re-incarnated other half); the only thing she is likely to fracture is the wishbone on a Christmas turkey; she is not likely to climb out of a window (unless there is a fire at home and she cannot reach the front door), and as for having to check her observations monthly, she remains pretty confident that she will know when she is dead.

Dora has her own teeth (sorry, Clark, don't mean to rub it in), neither arthritis nor osteoporosis is on the cards just yet, and if she *were* to complete her own 'body map' she would draw herself on the front and her hubby on the back. Her aim would be to confuse the hell out of her carers when they tried to figure out where to apply the creams.

In respect of medication, the only pill Dora has ever taken is no longer necessary as at her age the only thing she is likely to bear from now on is a grudge.

Dora is terminally ridden with idiocy. She may need to be heavily sedated on home-made cocktails, and as for depriving her of water, she assures us that she does not like it anyway.

Hmm maybe we (me, myself and Dora) do fit that end-of-life tick box after all, and as for being orientated to time and place – I know exactly where the story in my book is heading and hopefully it will land up in the right place.

The most important thing is that if only someone had asked ME what was really going on instead of presuming, everything could have run a lot more smoothly. In nursing, the old adage is that 'pain is whatever the patient says it is', but this notion should not be applied to this specific symptom at the detriment of all else.

# THE INVITATION

You might consider me the most insane and unlikely of people to become a detective, but there has been nothing secret about the way I have tried to handle my complaint as plain old 'me'. Yet at the risk of having to change my name by deed poll to avoid the risk of litigation, with Brooke as my pen-name I can confidently pick up my story at no risk to myself or my publisher.

So, correctly translated, and in going back to the Hungarian's hovercraft 'thing', it was *not* full of eels, although I have encountered many a slippery eel in the complaint system – people who have had this uncanny ability to avoid answering questions or take responsibility for their actions or inactions, instead deflecting the blame for what happened onto hubby himself.

As the smell of injustice still lingers inside my nostrils, these past years have been no picnic for me and whilst I embrace the 'angel image' that has been applied to nurses and doctors, not all angels have wings and some have very dirty faces (*Angels with Dirty Faces,* 1938) although I am not suggesting for one minute that the system has taken to employing dead-end kids just to fill the employment gap.

I salute the pillow-fluffing thing – it can make all the difference at times – but what I cannot advocate is that this should take precedence over the healthcare knowledge and life- saving skills that also come with the job.

I am as adamant now as I was five years ago that the prejudices which smokers and drinkers face on a daily basis when being admitted to hospital should not deter them from being treated as fairly as, say, someone who falls off a horse, breaks a leg and then needs surgeons to spend hours fixing them up. Equestrians know that every time they mount a horse there is the chance they might fall off – that horses can be the most unpredictable of creatures – yet still they ride. It is something they enjoy in life and have chosen to indulge in, fully aware of the risks.

One might say this woman doth protest too much when trying to justify how smoking and drinking can be good for anyone, especially as she is paid to be a good advocate for health promotion, but not everything in life is cut and dried.

So hubby caved in to his desire to self-medicate on fags and alcohol in spite of his best intentions to cut down; their seductive powers were so great that they got the better of him. His excuse was that these were the only vices he had, that he did not gamble away the housekeeping money nor resort to wife beating in a Rab C Nesbitt string vest.

To anyone who says they do not have an addiction that is bad for their health in one way or another, I would say 'Pinocchio.' I like hot curries and the short-term reward of capsaicin burn and endorphin release that goes with them. But the more I have eaten them, the more I have become addicted, to the point where other foods seem somewhat bland by comparison and I feel nutritionally dissatisfied.

Dopamine is the central chemical in our brain that regulates how we perceive and experience pleasure. I have never smoked, and whilst I joke about my drinking, my binges are few and far between. Hot food is *my* stimulant, *my* weakness, and whilst this too does not come without health risks such as upset stomach, nausea, dizziness and diarrhoea, I also have my own excuses for not wanting to give up, such as the antioxidant properties that can reduce the risk of me getting cancer, or the hope that eating enough turmeric might lower my chances of getting dementia. Furthermore, I have a cast iron stomach and have never suffered from Gandhi's revenge.

The government goes on about the drain on

resources of having to care for people with alcohol or smoking-related illnesses, yet the cost of serious injury to a rider is not limited to the time and resources needed to fix a spinal or head injury; it also involves the cost of long-term rehabilitation, psychological care and in many cases counselling, and all at the expense of the tax payer, as a result of *their* lifestyle choice. Yet they do not get treated with the same disregard and unsympathetic manner as someone who so readily might get diagnosed with cirrhosis of the liver when they have never touched a drop of alcohol (having non-alcoholic fatty liver disease for some other reason), or the person who needs treating for lung disease even though they have never smoked and finds themselves in the unfortunate situation of having respiratory problems, either due to second-hand smoke or work-related contaminants such as asbestos.

The point being that the brain or spinal injury an equestrian might face is as self-inflicted as any injury that a smoker or heavy drinker might face as a result of their lifestyle choices, yet it does not carry the same social stigma. So horse-riding might be seen as a posh person's sport, but it should not mean that the system must bow and scrape to their demands of fair treatment over anyone else. Tally Ho!

I rest my case.

I am not politically minded, any more than Alf Garnett was, but like him I like to call a spade a spade, so an addiction is an addiction, regardless of how it is channelled. We each of us have some guilty pleasure that might warrant medical attention at any stage.

'Justice delayed is justice denied' (William E Gladstone, 1809-1898), and equally so the poorer children who were denied free milk under the rule of the Iron Lady ('Thatcher the milk snatcher', who Alf claimed should have been chained to the bloody kitchen sink instead of running the country). So too, the chance of me getting a free investigation into hubby's death has been snatched away from me, and my own journey has also been nothing short of a comedy sketch.

But there is more than one way to cook an egg right (straight or posh), which is why I am formally inviting you to join me in a game of 'whodunit' in which I shall give you equal opportunity to try and help solve the mystery of how hubby may have come to die.

I will present to you all the clues that may eventually lead towards the prime 'suspects', if not the main culprit, in this very complex story.

Without any insight into the workings of the medical profession you may have difficulty in making links, but I shall do my utmost to translate what might seem complicated matters to you. Then you might then be able to digest the information a little more easily.

I have had this tendency in the past to soar outside the realms of reality, but in this instance, and whilst I seek to solve the 'crime' as I see it both sensibly and scientifically in terms of evidence base, I cannot promise that I shall not still crack a joke or two along the way. This is my coping mechanism. It does not mean I have stopped grieving.

All being well then, perhaps we will meet at the

moral crossroads and exchange thoughts over a cup of my finest tea. Have no fear, it will not be all doom and gloom. I shall not put you on the spot so that you are faced with the dilemma of having to decide who, if anyone, should be left begging and screaming for mercy on their way to the electric chair and face being given a lethal injection. I just need you to listen to a few hard-hitting truths.

Virtually visit each location, and consider the clues. Take note of each person's involvement. Try then to imagine in your mind any details on the medical records as I describe them to you.

This is not a game about me trying to 'point score', but one that has the potential to be played out across the field, even though no two cases will be the same.

# ALL WHISTLE AND NO WILLPOWER

—∞—

First I need to build up a character profile, so you will be able to remember who is who as the plot thickens, starting with the victim, or should I say, the corpse (sorry my love)!

You have probably gathered by now that I do not dismiss or hide the fact that hubby enjoyed a drink or two, but it should not be assumed that he was any more alcohol or fag-dependent than any of the fictitious TV cops (i.e. Bergerac, Poirot or that one in the crumpled coat) who instead were depicted as being cheekily suave.

His lordship did depend on me to make sure the fridge was always well stocked with his favourite tipple, which he looked forward to after a hard day's work, and trust me he had no problem drinking it, but if that classed him as being drink dependent, then feel free to read into it what you will.

Equally, did anyone poo-poo Paul Newman's right arm action in his starring role in *Fort Apache, The Bronx* (1981), as the hard-drinking veteran cop whose excuse was that he had to contend with fighting crime in one of the poorest and most run-down precincts in New York? Of course not! It pulled in a tidy sum for the producers back then, and if Mr Newman was left handed then I stand corrected.

Now I am in no way suggesting for one minute that hubby worked in a decaying or impoverished part of the county in which *we* lived, but characteristically, in his role as a police officer, he, like all those fictitious cops, and inclusive as a real life British 'bobby', he did occupy a special role in society. Over time my beloved had been exposed to all sorts of dangers, especially in his younger days, many of which had the potential to be life-threatening, yet, he had to plod on complying with the demands of his superiors even though he may not always have seen eye to eye with them, and was always the one that the officers under his command went to when things got tough or when they were on the brink of suicide as he climbed up the ranks.

Both drinking and smoking by TV detectives, especially in our heyday, had always been seen as the mark of a man.

'Who loves you baby?'

'You do,' I told him, 'but I wish you would get rid of the lollipop and grow some hair.' (*Kojak,* 1973-1978)

I was joking of course.

My own 'partner in crime' had an adequate head of hair for the best part, and watching him cringe when sucking on a lolly from a sherbet dib-dab *was* rather amusing in someone so grown up. It would remind me of the joke about a mother-in-law being so ugly that when she sucked a lemon it was the lemon that pulled the face. Sorry Mum! Love you really.

Or of the time when hubby told me that I had a 'sweet face', only to have then gone and ruined it by following through with, 'like a chewed-up toffee.' But that was him all over. Some might have taken offence, but not me – it was just a laugh.

Hubby had tried on so many occasions to give up the fags having sampled tablets, chewing gum and nicotine patches along the way, but as we have established, smoking was something he enjoyed. Besides, he had also become addicted to collecting the Rothman's tokens that we could then exchange for gifts that we probably wouldn't have bought in the first place, even at discount. I can still picture them coming through the post.

I don't know how many times I heard him say, 'I will try and cut down in the New Year.' 'After all, tomorrow is another day' I would think to myself – every single day, in fact – as we lived that non-Hollywood existence.

In the period of adjustment between crime

prevention and retirement, hubby had a lot of time on his hands. There was no denying that he drank more, until the novelty of being home all day wore off. I have said it before and I say it again, alcohol did, in some small way, work as a cheap anaesthetic to numb the fact that he no longer felt as 'purposeful' as he once did, nor felt he would ever be held in such high esteem in the public eye again, especially as he had not planned on retiring then.

# BOARD TO DEATH

—⊷∞⊶—

As both a novice writer and a nurse, there is a huge burden of responsibility resting upon my shoulders to uphold ethical standards in each case, especially in relation to confidentiality and data protection; although in the writer's world, this would be more adhering to the copyright laws and anonymity.

How shall I tackle this sensitive issue then?

I know. Who likes board games?

Not me. I get 'board' *with* them easily, except for a few exceptions, but there are times when they can come in handy, such as now. With a little inspiration you may not yet have a 'Cluedo' as to how this fits in with my nonsense, but all will be revealed.

Ironically, and in keeping with the tradition of *that* game, there were six likely culprits instrumental in hubby's demise, and not a professor, a colonel or reverend in sight. Instead there was a GP, a nurse, a clinician, a consultant, an anaesthetist and a Chief Executive, to whom I shall refer as the 'suspects', whether their involvement in his care was direct or indirect.

You will also encounter a couple of other very important people who cannot go without mention, they being the pathologist, the Coroner's Officer and the Coroner himself.

I have had to be my own private detective over the years. I have been more than patient. I am trained in clinical nursing to a degree and I had been very watchful of how things had progressed through the use of virtual reality.

Temporary self-diagnoses with 'mixamygamesup' - I have the 'Monopoly' on the creation of this bizarre courtroom drama, which I hope you will enjoy.

So as that lonely widow detective, I feel quite excited about sharing my investigation with you all from the setting up of my 'office', spotting the clues, gathering evidence including laboratory findings, misleading evidence, suspect identification and questioning, detecting forged documents, and finally measuring things up.

My first inclination was to use the word 'suspects' when setting out to introduce you to the players in the game, but since a 'suspect' is someone who is thought to have committed a crime, at this stage you do not know anything for sure, so I shall instead refer to them as 'persons of interest.' They are:

The GP or general practitioner, whose job is to take responsibility for providing preventive care and routine treatment and where issues relative to his/her patient's illness falls outside of his 'expertise' he is required to refer them onto a more specialist doctor.

The nurse, who is responsible primarily for keeping an eye on each and every aspect of a patient under his/her care, including observing and recording vital signs, diagnosing illness by analysing symptoms, and taking the required actions to aid recovery.

The nurse is further responsible for providing instant care in a medical emergency, such as a heart attack; giving out medication as prescribed by the medical professionals; adhering to the protocols, rules and regulations in regard to record-keeping among other things; and for being able to recognise and respond to patient deterioration through liaison with other members of the healthcare team.

The hospital clinician is a doctor who works in clinical practice as opposed to in a GP surgery. He/she must practice medicine using an evidence base and follow the professional codes of conduct set both in law and by his/her regulatory body in order to keep his/her licence to practise medicine. It is imperative that they carry out physical examinations as a patient's illness and medical history dictates.

The consultant is a clinician with more seniority who will have undertaken training in a specialist field of medicine. Responsible not only for the clinical 'happenings' on their wards and for the administration side, their role also extends to the management of the junior doctors serving under them.

The anaesthetist is a medical practitioner responsible for sedating a patient, especially where intubating is necessary to help them breathe more easily and where a packet of Tunes does not do the trick (Wrigley Company). They have an added responsibility to make sure the tube is in the right place, because if it is not, and it moves, then the cells in the person's brain will start to die through lack of oxygen. This is referred to as hypoxia – a life-changing and potentially fatal event.

Selecting the right anaesthetic agents is paramount, as without a thorough knowledge of how each drug works in relation to another the patient could suffer an adverse reaction, deteriorate or even die.

If there was any kind of manager within the department, then he/she did not come forward with any explanations – the manager being the person who should be ultimately responsible for the clinical management of everyone on the 'shop floor' or department if you like, to ensure that standards of quality are being maintained. The one who must work closely with the senior medical and nursing staff and assume accountability for any failings by those employed in the department, especially where a patient's life has been put at risk or worse still, they have died whether expected or not. Each departmental manager reports to the Chief Executive .

The pathologist is the person responsible for carrying out post mortems and for interpreting and diagnosing changes in the body as a result of disease or trauma. He or she will look at tissue samples under a microscope and report on the findings. All you really need to know about a pathologist is that all post mortems he/she carries out will be on dead people!

Then there is the Coroner's Officer, whose principle role is to act as representative of the HM Coroner (the bigger wig) in the investigation of any death referred to him and to make enquiries into potential findings of 'treasure'.

In my case, an Aladdin's cave would seem to be a more apt description. Just as the pathologist could not have carried out the post mortem on hubby without opening him up, the Coroner's Officer could not have banked for one minute on my opening up a Pandora's box, simply because if this had been a suspected manslaughter case in any other context than by clinical negligence as I saw it, a police investigation would have been carried out and no stone would have been left unturned. However, with little knowledge of the different types of medicines and how they might interact, or of the workings of the different types of medical professionals in general, the true extent of any alleged crime is not so easy for a coroner to determine.

The purpose of a criminal investigation is to gather evidence to identify a suspect and support an arrest, which may involve an exploratory inspection of a person or property. Linked to that there is also the need for the police to look into a probable cause – the standard proof required for that 'exploratory' search – to be undertaken in the first place, meaning that evidence of criminality can be found in a specific place based on what facts or apparent facts are available at the time.

In a clinical context, when someone dies unexpectedly in hospital the 'person' should be substituted with the 'patient' and the 'specific place' should be interpreted as the hospital where this is a known fact. Evidence to determine criminality, or not, should be relative to medical notes (written evidence), and a probable cause of death should not deviate from this.

'Exploratory inspection' in the medical world should come from internal sources (staff – managerial or otherwise), health regulators (such as the Care Quality Commission), or any other bodies responsible for overseeing good medical practice.

As my jurors it is vitally important that you consider both sides of the same judicial coin. I had thought about inviting Inspector Morse and his side-kick Lewis along for the ride, but since they tend to drink more than they should during their heavy work schedules (although I blame their producers for this), I cannot be sure that they would be able to act with 'sober objectivity'.

So what of the Coroner himself then? He is the one whose job it is to determine who the deceased was and how, when and where they came by their death. Where it is suspected that the death had been sudden and from an 'unknown cause', for example, he may request that a post mortem be carried out, as well as an inquest, especially where there is conflicting or complex evidence about the circumstances surrounding it.

In my dealings with the Coroner leading up to the inquest I never had the pleasure of meeting him face to face – contact was only through Royal Mail. I have no idea whether or not he fitted the typical 'profile' of coroners I have watched on the box, who are generally cast as middle-aged and cynical, ones that tend to mock the afflicted and blame the deceased for not having conformed to life's norms. In typical movie style this is so that they can reach a nice tidy conclusion, but whether fictitiously or not, they are the last hope of justice for the bereaved.

I really hope he goes against the grain, else I shall be doing him a huge injustice.

The manner of hubby's injury was not a freak of nature, the nature of his injury was not a 'flattened spirit', and he did not leave this world to play where the goblins went (*Wizard of Oz*, 1939), yet there was still no proper explanation as to what really happened to have caused him to have died so unexpectedly, as the post mortem revealed.

So now you have met the characters. Since a number of years have now elapsed, with the exception of one character who sticks in my mind, in order to keep things interesting I shall try to stir your imagination through a little manipulation. My heart may be bleeding, but seeking to stab everyone in the back in the looks department is not very grown up, so I may depict some of them to be more beautiful than others.

Next I shall move on to the 'weapons,' or should I say the different types of 'instruments' that may have been responsible for hubby's injuries. Bear in mind, if you will, that an 'instrument' does not necessarily have to be a visible object – other things can be instrumental in the shape of things, so which might have been responsible for causing harm or indeed for having delivering the final blow?

The possibilities are:

The *inappropriate* medication prescribed at the GP surgery (the Make-me-wait Medical Centre) before hubby went to hospital

- The clinician's failure to carry out diagnostic testing into suspected internal bleeding on admission to hospital.

- The contradiction in diagnoses, by which proper treatment was delayed at a crucial time, treatment that could have prevented an untoward incident.

- The failings by senior clinicians to check blood results during a time of critical illness before moving hubby from a safe zone to a general ward.

- The delay by the night nurse to act upon the National Early Warning Score.

- The delay by the night nurse to report the abnormal ECG readings higher up the chain.

- The inappropriate medication given pre-arrest and based on assumption.

- The inappropriate medication given post-arrest, following a misdiagnosis

- The inappropriate use of and incorrect amounts of sedation during intubation.
- The failure to use rescue medication when the level of hubby's sedation was deeper than initially intended.

It is only because the hospital operates a 'zero tolerance' policy that I can rest assured that hubby had not met his fate at the sharp end of a dagger, a lead pipe, a revolver or a spanner. Candlesticks too are not permitted on the wards, so that rules them out.

As for the rope thing, I remained quietly confident that, in time, as the lies continued, all those who were responsible for looking after his lordship might just have enough of it to hang themselves.

Next let us consider the rooms in which the 'injuries' had probably been sustained. This was no luxury hospital, so you can rule out a billiard room, a ballroom or a library, leaving only:

- The GP surgery
- The Assessment Unit
- The High Dependency Unit
- The Intensive Care Unit
- The Resuscitation Theatre
- The anaesthetists 'office'
- The medical ward
- Some other ward

It is a bad writer, I know, who gives away the end of a story before the reader has finished the beginning, but one thing I am sure you have already concluded is that the love of my life ended up in the 'cellar', better known as the morgue.

It was impossible for hubby to have self-navigated around the place – the porters took him to his various destinations. Staff appeared to make the rules up as they went along and as for note-taking, it was more a case of note altering – another contentious issue.

My other half was a one off – my 'limited edition' - but let us not kid ourselves that clinical negligence cases fall short of this. They are making headlines every day, yet rarely do those left to pick up the pieces get resolution, due to legal privileges.

# NARRATIVELY SPEAKING

—◦∞◦—

I wait with bated breath to see how many of you will make up my jury. It will depend of course on how many of you are reading my book right now and are keen to indulge in my game of deductive reasoning. Perhaps you are in the medical game yourself, in which case your opinions might be based on intuition. You might even be in the police game, in which case I should value your opinion even more.

I am hopeful for 12 sympathetic women at least, although *12 Angry Men* (1957) who have lost their wives under similar circumstances will serve my purpose equally well.

This will not involve having to roll a dice that may land on a specific person, weapon or location or that you should have to painstakingly move around a folded board, so this is a relatively simple game of find the culprit.

So when you are ready, get your quilled pens and reporters' notebooks out as I summarise what I had complained out all those years ago. In the words of that popular 1950s/1960s American singer Dion (Mr DiMucci), 'Here's my story sad but true, about a boy that I once knew', except my own real-life lover did not 'take my love and run around with every girl in town' – just me. My book may not have the makings of a Hollywood movie, but I have a character (hubby) and a mission (to seek justice), and along with the many conflicts along the way, I feel I have adequately mastered the art of writing a synopsis.

I shall start at the beginning, build up the suspense and finish with the punchline – or at least that is my intention; to put things in the right order.

## Synopsis

This is a story about a man who went to his GP twice in less than a month to seek something for his back pain. He was given two different types of extremely strong painkillers. Neither doctor had properly considered his medical history and existing medications when prescribing these new drugs. Just as he always followed the instructions on the lighter fluid container that he used to fill up his Ronson lighter, so too the man would have carefully adhered to the instructions of his own GP or associates when it came to taking medication. He would also have adhered to the patient leaflet by doing 'exactly what it said on the tin'. OK, so that was Ronseal's advertising slogan, but you get my drift.

Over time the man began to feel unwell, having fainted on at least two occasions for no particular or obvious reason while on holiday. There had been several bouts of nausea, his appetite had dwindled, and he had experienced unusual breathlessness. Having been referred to hospital by his GP when he turned up at the surgery one morning looking decidedly pale, extremely dizzy and with a blood pressure reading that was practically in his boots, the doc was concerned he might have internal bleeding, so he referred him to his local hospital. However, at no point in time was an investigation into that possible bleed carried out, and without anything to confirm or deny this the medical staff based their opinion on what they had read from his GP letter, having crossed off their initial suspicions of infection and replaced it with something else. Antibiotics were prescribed, but they were not the right ones for the job.

Over the following five days the man became little more than a human pincushion for the medical vampires, yet despite the blood results and other pathology tests pointing to the fact that he was 'an accident waiting to happen', there appeared to be a high level of concordance between the clinicians as to what they presumed the diagnosis to be. Critical time was lost in which a full recovery could have been made, but that was not to be.

Despite his seriously abnormal blood test results, the man was moved at an unearthly hour, without warning, from the Intensive Care Unit where he was already being monitored for changes in his condition. Soon after the transfer he felt unwell, complaining of chest pain, A diagnostic test was carried out which pointed to the likelihood of a heart attack, but that result was not reported to anyone in higher authority.

Medication given over an hour later triggered a respiratory arrest. Having been misdiagnosed, he was again given drugs that added insult to that injury both at the pre and post-arrest stages, which required the man to be sedated and intubated and attached to a machine to help him breathe. Hope was lost that the man would come out of the induced coma as a series of suspected medical mishaps ensued, and as a result his family had to witness his oxygen machine being turned off.

The hospital staff openly admitted that they could not be clear as to the cause of the man's death, despite their previous speculation. The man was not terminally ill and there was nothing to suggest that he needed any aggressive treatment when he went for a routine check-up.

The Coroner asked a pathologist to carry out a post mortem, and when the deceased man's wife contested the cause of death in which smoking and drinking were described as 'contributory factors' and 'likely' causative; the pathologist's 'opinion' being based on 'the information that was available at the time' – that being little more than an account of this man's past medical history, which the Trust were only too delighted to highlight.

The interim death certificate issued six days after her husband's death however stated that 'the *precise* medical cause of death has not yet been ascertained' as an inquest was opened and adjourned pending further investigation into the evidence that the wife had produced to support her concerns. The inquest was not re-opened until 14 months later.

There was no jury present at the inquest, as the Coroner did not consider that anyone was on trial. Only a handful of carefully selected clinicians were asked to attend the court discussion. By this time they remembered little of the man in question and their pre-inquest statements only 'touched' on his death. Most of the information about the care and treatment he had received, especially regarding his medication, had seemingly and selectively been 'brushed over', despite the extensive lengths his wife had gone to in order to support her allegations of negligence.

The clinicians, in keeping with the Coroner's rules, would have had the option not to answer any questions in which they might incriminate themselves, and conveniently an inquest procedure did not permit that any of the witnesses could be cross-examined either. The man's family did not attend the inquest for personal reasons.

The narrative verdict afterwards concluded that the man had died a 'natural' death – multi-organ failure. In the closing statement of the verdict, the Coroner wrote that whilst her husband had been admitted to the hospital as a result of being dizzy and short of breath, for which he was then given a course of antibiotics to 'address a concern over a possible infection', there was 'no evidence to suggest he had liver failure That it was 'not clear' as to how the man's health had resulted in a dramatic and sudden decline resulting in him developing multi-organ failure.

The man's wife was convinced from the start that her husband had died from sepsis (a dangerous immune response caused by an infection), whether as a result of infection, drug-induced or some other trauma, but nobody was prepared to consider any oversights. The results of the blood and other pathology test results are not works of fiction but seek to support very real concerns.

Now a widow, the man's wife remained unconvinced that her husband's death should have been deemed to be from 'natural causes' and questioned why a toxicology test had not been carried out. It took her several years to discover the reason for this. The fact that the Coroner had been told by the clinicians that his death was a result of an 'underlying condition', was therefore not reported as a serious untoward incident, so it did not trigger an internal investigation in which a root cause analysis could have taken place. This allowed everything from the Trust's perspective to be wrapped up in a nice neat package with bows on.

The man's widow vowed to get to the bottom of

things, no matter how long it took, as the lies and inconsistencies in report writing flowed outside the realms of the Trust. She had sought further help to no avail and the cause of death had been based on little more on opinions, likelihoods and suggestions as to how her husband might have died at every turn. The wife's concerns about him having been moved from the intensive care unit to a normal ward hours before he died, upon which he had 'become unwell during the early hours complaining of chest pain and shortness of breath upon which he then arrested (pulseless electrical activity) and whereby after approximately 4 cycles of cardiopulmonary resuscitation and adrenaline, cardiac output was resumed even though oxygen levels remained low' (Coroner's narrative), were even more compounded as, in the Coroner's words, her husband's 'condition deteriorated as organs were showing signs of shutting down' and that 'following his cardiac arrest and after the withdrawal of support' he died in hospital that evening.

The man's widow was adamant that multi-organ failure does not happen for no apparent reason, and that has been the basis of her quest for answers and the truth behind what may or may not have happened to have brought about that unfortunate event.

In the world of policing, the equivalent of a synopsis would be an investigation or incident report. It could be argued that an officer might come over as uneducated or stupid to those who he or she might call upon to decide the guilt or innocence of a suspect if his or her reports were full of misspelled words or grammatical errors. In turn this might then reflect badly on their superiors, if they had signed the statements off without actually having read them, which in a court of law would leave them with egg on their face.

For the purpose of my 'court hearing' however, it is definitely my intention to mix up or make up words, whether grammatically correct or not, as I want us to have fun along the way, so do not blame my editor who, after all, would have read this fully before allowing it to go to print.

How is it that I can write such a detailed synopsis, I hear you say? That is because 'I was that lady and he was my man, whenever he reached for me I tried to do all that I could but I was heading to somewhere, somewhere I'd never been, but I was never frightened and I was ready to fight through the power of love'. (Jennifer Rush, 1984)

# MISTAKEN IDENTITY

Suspects in a crime always seem to have a hideout. There are many definitions, but the one I like the most is 'a safe place of hiding, especially from the law.' When crooks know detectives are looking for them they hide in places where they will not be found, but what if that hideout was full of many faces in the biggest of crowds, such as the setting in my synopsis, where they all seemed to dress similarly, uniformly even?

But instead of running from the law in the same way as your traditional crook, and from my own reckoning, a medic's hiding place is behind the 'duty of candour' and the Bolam Test – their 'get out of jail free' cards, as I see it, which they can lay out so cleverly and expertly on the table as proof that they acted within the law.

For the record, the Bolam Test is a tool used to assess medical negligence. In brief, it seeks to agree that in law there should be a duty of care between a doctor and a patient, yet by the same token it goes on to say that standards of care are 'a matter of medical judgement'. The crux of the matter is that 'a doctor cannot be found negligent if he acted in accordance with a practice accepted as 'proper' by a reasonable body of medical 'men' skilled in that particular art or merely because someone else (another 'body of opinion') might take a contrary view'.

I wish Bert, our Border Collie, were still alive today, because he could help me with a little 'nose work.' As his faithful friend, hubby used to give Bert the opportunity to have an outlet for his natural scenting ability, and our crazy canine would get so excited when hubby used to hide his socks or other objects behind pieces of furniture around the home. In one of his unique extended roles hubby was used to working alongside search dogs trained to sniff out explosives, and whilst he would take Bert to work with him on the odd occasion, as a family pet, he was just as astute at being able to indicate a 'find' and would most certainly be able to sniff out any contradictions in this case.'

Whether in the police world or the clinical field, expert opinion is vitally important in assisting the courts to decide whether or not the person on 'trial' had exercised a proper level of skill that befitted the circumstances of the case. In policing, a detective working on a case might call to the witness stand a handwriting expert (a graphologist) for example, to back up their case in a law court where someone has been accused of forgery, whereas a lawyer defending a doctor in a clinical negligence case might call for an expert medical opinion. However, despite expert testimony the law will have us believe that it must be the court that decides whether or not standards of care have been achieved, not that medical expert. Yet there have been those who have taken it upon themselves to side with their own internal adjudicators.

Bearing all this in mind, I need you, my helpers, to consider whether the GPs in the first instance had acted in accordance with proper practice as laid down by the General Medical Council; whether all the anaesthetists at the hospital would have given anyone else the same combination of sedatives; whether other clinicians would have considered it appropriate for medical files to have important information crossed out or written over without explanation; and whether any other nurses would have felt it OK to wait until a doctor happened to be doing his/her rounds before bothering them about an abnormal ECG reading.

Again, I am only touching on matters of opinion, just as the coroner had touched on the death of hubby at the inquest and whilst much of the issues around clinical negligence is based on 'intention to do harm' – if a crook told a detective he did not mean to forge someone's signature on a cheque to completely wipe them out of billions of pounds (financial 'harm' right?,) or a burglar did not mean to go into someone's house and steal all their valuable possessions saying he thought it was where the three bears lived and that all he was really after was a bowl of porridge yet had succumbed to temptation once he saw a jewellery box lying open, would this wash with the courts and get them off? I think not.

But what of medical staff who seek to cover up their actions when someone dies? Why should they be entitled to that 'get out of jail free' card that the Bolam Test in essence imitates? And why should there be no time limit imposed on the police within which to solve a crime if more evidence is needed, yet even with all the evidence someone could possibly have in a case of clinical negligence, if things are not wrapped up within three years then that must be the end of it.

The Firchester, I feel, is as good a name as any for a hospital, using Belinda Ward's fictitious creation of that British spin-off for the more familiar Sesame Street as my inspiration and in maintaining confidentiality. At that hotel of a similar name, those who run it seek ways in which to resolve any issues their guests encounter during their stay. In the same way, we expected that those responsible for working at the hospital should have sought at early admission to solve the matter of hubby's apparent and suspected symptoms as a 'guest' also.

To say the hospital was run by a bunch of muppets

at this stage would be unfair. That is for you, the jurors, to decide.

Oh, and I ought to give hubby a name, I think, so he will seem more real to you. It will need to be short and sweet (like me, so I have been told). How about Ted? You like it? Good, Ted it is then.

My account of what happened following Ted's visit to the quacks is neither absurd nor exaggerated in any way. I seek to tell my story in a light-hearted way for no other reason than that I want you to leave my book entertained if not enlightened, despite the sorry tale it tells.

'I solemnly swear I am up to *all* good.' Please keep this in mind readers – that I am writing for the benefit of the public at large and accordingly I shall try to simplify the medical vocabulary as much as possible, else you will get stressed, anxious even, which will limit your ability to listen and learn.

In having been given unlawful access to information about Ted by his GP, which had nothing to do with his immediate problem, not only had his possession rights been breached but as a result I maintain that poor judgements in care were made that could not then be reversed. This started from the minute he was admitted to hospital and that unnecessary information was handed over to them. That deviated away from the potential bleeding, which was ignored.

'Friends, Romans, non-Romans, country folk and those of you living in suburbia, lend me your eyes,' I say, seated behind my keyboard. I should like to bury those people, not praise them, for overlooking the plain, simple facts. The failure by those doctors to discharge their obligation to carry out necessary investigations in an unbiased and non-presumptive way is essentially a tortuous liability. Given the length of time the management and clinicians at the Firchester took to respond to my concerns,' tortoise' liability would be a more apt definition.

In hindsight I am thinking that perhaps now is not a good time to use the word 'bury.' Joking or otherwise, no doubt there is some clause in criminal law that would make this constitute threatening behaviour, but there again my 'persons of interest' deserve more than a slap on the wrists, so unless Mark Antony wants to re-write his script then I shall be rebellious (like Caesar) and stick to my guns.

Griffith (2001) suggests that legal outcomes are not based on 'truth' but on 'proof' and the only thing I have been interested in is justice – not hand-outs.

In the words of singer Jessie J, 'It's not about the money, money, money, I don't need their money, money, money' - but I do wonder how they sleep at night and why they continue to act so god damn mysterious.

As for 'everyone looking to the left, and everyone looking to the right' – I wonder if they have even looked over their shoulders for one minute whilst I have been wrestling with the anger at their false dialogues.

Now I do not confess to having a halo, halo, halo and the 'tit-for-tat' thing would only point my moral compass in the wrong direction and I need to stay focused. My dad always used to say there was more than one way to skin a cat. My siblings and I used to cringe every time he used that expression, but as we got older it painted a less gruesome picture.

'More than one method used to accomplish the same end' is a nicer 'take' on this, I feel, so I shall attempt several different ways to help you come to your decision as to how clinical mistakes can come about and how this may have happened in Ted's case.

As a young child growing up in that council flat, in North London in the 1960's (not as Brooke but plain old me), I recall what I could only describe as an awful stench coming from the kitchen. Having sailed the oceans between Liverpool and Calcutta as a merchant seaman during the time of the British Raj, it was a delicacy that my nan used to enjoy, and something that Dad would cook for her at home visits having watched it being cooked first hand on the streets that lined the Ganges rivers. Dad saw it as bringing a bit of Howrah to Haringey, and as the eldest I was more open than my siblings to experiencing different tastes from afar.

For the best part of my childhood and into my early teens I came to recognise the pungent smell of Bombay duck – the 'meat' that had a distinctive taste of its own, until I later learned that it was not a duck at all, it was in fact a heavily dried and salted *fish*; a lizardfish actually.

I took everything with a pinch of salt (excuse the pun) in those days, because as a child I had neither the knowhow nor the assertiveness to want to challenge how it could be called one thing yet taste like another. My parents were not trying to pull the wool over my eyes, but I soon learned not to take things at face value.

As I recall, and irrespective of what it was called, it tasted quite nice apart from the smell. Mum would try desperately to apologise to Nan for the undiplomatic way in which my siblings had held their noses with a 'phwah', 'phwah', and a 'what's that horrible stink, Mummy?'

Just as this delicacy was banned by the European Commission in 1997, a British businessman reportedly won the right to have it reinstated after a four-year campaign. He had apparently used the MP route to take it to the High Commission and won his case.

So where is all this going, I can hear you ask, and what on earth has Bombay duck got to do with my story?

Bombay duck comes in two forms, fresh and dried, and although their odours differ slightly and there are differences in the way they might be eaten, they are in fact one and the same species.

Just as I had misinterpreted what I was eating back then, after hubby died I misinterpreted the complaint system and the coronial justice system to be one that was based on fairness for all irrespective of the circumstances, but the smell of Father's fish is nothing compared to the stench of secrecy and lies that has surrounded me ever since. I went down the MP route when trying to take things to the top also. You will have to wait till the end of the book to see how that panned out.

If only I could get hold of some of that fish today, I should be interested to see how others might interpret it – whether they might diagnose it in the same way as I did or come up with the correct answer.

My dad used to joke that if you stuck some steam from a kettle into an old jam jar, put a lid on and told an American tourist it was English fog, they would be queuing up to buy it. I am just saying – they did buy the wrong bridge, after all!

My dad, bless him, was the most sceptical person I knew – perhaps I had inherited the sceptic streak equally as much as these days I joke about having inherited the 'Mallen streak' as the grey is beginning to show through the parting of my chestnut hair (Catherine Cookson).

One might say 'meat, fish, what the hell – it is still Bombay duck.' Equally one might say 'steam from a kettle, real fog, what the hell – it is still cloudy air.'

I find this a little discerning – they might be perceived as being the same thing based on sight alone if someone does not put them right. But would it be morally right or ethical to keep s*chtumm* at their expense? I personally think not.

'Mirror, mirror on the wall, who is the nit-pickiest of them all?'

But am I really, or is it right that I should be concerned with details that I feel are significant? It has not been my intention to find fault yet fault cannot be found where it does not truly lie, now can it?

Consider for one moment, jurors, this case of 'mistaken identity.'

In hospital, unknown to him, a patient is given cottage pie instead of shepherd's pie (not that they ordinarily would have the luxury of an either/or option, unless they were paying through the nose of course!)

Now these dishes might be considered one and the same – minced meat under creamy mashed potato – but what would happen, I wonder, if that person happened to be a Hindu, for example, and became ill as a result of having eaten something that was 'alien' to him? Leave aside the psychological guilt of having eaten beef instead of lamb. Don't worry folks, I am not about to go into a lecture on ethnicity. I want you to think about the potential for malpractice.

Healthcare organisations have a duty to incorporate cultural diversity into their organisation's culture but in this instance, where the organisation had failed to take patient A's needs into account, it might also be considered that they had failed to provide him with comprehensive quality person-centred care, and I have no doubt there would be some clause within the Human Rights Act (1998) whereby his case would qualify for a free hearing and financial remedy for any 'distress' caused.

The Trust might try to defend their actions by saying that the pies are, in essence, the same thing, but they are not, and a good lawyer in human rights issues might argue that they had failed to take into account his cultural needs and had breached his right to have his cultural preference respected.

Is there not the same potential for the argument of missed diagnoses and misdiagnoses? Yet in hubby's case where the outcome proved to be fatal, according to Article 2 of that same Act, he had a right to life. The discrimination he faced as a smoker and a drinker, did not warrant the same respect.

Diversity in care is no longer about religious or cultural differences. There are so many other spectra that come under this umbrella term, and they include respect for someone's lifestyle choices. Where healthcare professionals fail to embrace this concept, the provision of quality nursing care is just not there.

# THE COURTYARD

Which of you out there remembers, as I do, breaking the 'no-ball-games allowed' rule in a council estate courtyard? All of us who lived in ours were good kids, and our behaviour was always very 'sociable.' The signs were not enforceable then, any more than they have been fifty years on, and it is with some amusement that I read only the other day that Haringey 'bosses' had recruited the services of ex-England defender Ledley King to help in the removal of such signs across the London Borough.

Somewhat ironic, don't you think? Perhaps he might like a kick around first just to see what it feels like to be a poor kid!

So 'Queenie, Queenie, who's got the ball' and 'Please mother may I' were the ball games responsible for turning me into a rebel and, sitting here today tapping away like this about serious, grown-up stuff, I could well be accused of having lost the plot here as much as in my previous novel, although I can assure you I have not and it is all relevant.

We were always taught to say 'please', which is why this became our adopted name for it all those years ago, and it just rolls of my tongue naturally nowadays. And the 'name of that game' literally was that one of us was appointed to be 'mother' - the one who had the power to grant or dismiss the other kid's wishes in a bid to move closer and closer to her from a short distance away her using all sorts of funny moves in a bid to reach her first and therefore be the winner. 'Mother' would be the one to stand firm, stare the kids in the eye and give out her own instructions, just to make things more difficult. Alternatively the kid picked to be 'Queenie' would have to turn her back on the rest of us and throw a ball over his/her shoulder whilst the rest of the kids tried to catch it or pick it up and then hide it somewhere on their person.

In a bid to fool 'Queenie', everyone regardless had to put their hands behind their backs so she would not know who actually had the ball. It was then a game of elimination as the kids set about asking her whether the one who had it was short or tall, hairy or bald; but in that we used to cheat and pass the ball to each other behind her back in a bid to outwit her.

Having assumed the role of 'mother', as well as the wife, in the complaint, system I needed no one's permission to take a step forward towards the hospital's patient liaison service when trying to find out what had happened to my hubby. I felt like Oliver Twist holding out an empty bowl. I was hungry for answers.

Explanations from the start were very poor – they in no way satisfied my need. 'Please sirs, I want some more' I would ask with each letter that I wrote to the Chief Executive, giving her every opportunity to be honest and up front with me. However, I was not on her list of priorities and found myself time and time again back at the starting point.

Just as we kids had tried to avoid 'Queenie' learning who really had the ball, so too the 'queen' of the complaint system, took no steps towards trying to find out exactly who was responsible for hubby's eventual death, aware that the buck would lie with her. Her role did not require any visible leadership on the 'shop floor' (wards) it seemed that role was little more than seeking to act at all times in the interests of her organisation and not to compromise it in any way, instead hiding behind her legal department before attempting to respond to my letters of concern, even though she was not medically trained and did not have one iota about the matter I was contesting.

*Primum non nocere* (first do no harm) is a principle I frequently use. How often over the years have I wanted to shake the shoulders of all those in the medical profession who had failed Ted and shout 'what was wrong with you all – did you learn nothing at medical school?' *Primum non nocere* forms part of the original Hippocratic Oath which physicians swear to uphold specific ethical standards. OK, so they may not have to wave a magic wand to swear their allegiance to the medical profession and they may not have to have their registration numbers tattooed on their arms so that they light up under UV rays, but nevertheless it is something that they should take seriously and I am sure, in most cases this is true.

The Hypocritical Oath I felt was a more apt translation in Ted's case. Two words that can sound so similar yet are so different in meaning. The original oath has since been superseded by the British General Medical's Good Medical Practice Guide, in which breaches of any codes under the General Medical Council can result in doctors losing their licence to practice or face disciplinary action, although the onus of proof always seems to rest with the unsatisfied 'customer'.

The British National Formulary, or BNF as it is often called, is a kind of 'bible' used by doctors, GPs and specialist practitioners, containing an extensive list of medications available on prescription and advising on the correct doses to give, any likely interactions with other medications and possible side effects of those medications, but more importantly any indications for prescribing or not as each individual person's circumstances dictate. First published in 1949, it continues to be published twice yearly, the last one having been issued as the 73rd edition in March 2017, just in case you are curious. Pop into most pharmacies and they will let you have the previous one for nothing, although I shall take no responsibility if you should all turn into hypochondriacs on account of information overload.

This heavy little paperback may well come in handy for you later on.

# NEWS HEADLINES

———⋈———

So Ted dealt with matters of law as opposed to my affiliation with lancets, but there is a point where the two disciplines tend to cross over, particularly where terminology is concerned.

In my altered ego state and in true detective form I like to think I am quick-witted, sharp-eyed and always on the lookout for anything remotely suspicious, knowing that the most unlikely of things may lead to important clues. Consider for one moment the word WIFE. For the average bod this will be taken to mean one who has been appointed through holy matrimony – a title I held in high esteem. However, hubby's own interpretation of this was a mnemonic – Washing, Ironing, F*****g, Etc. Well I came up trumps when it came to laundering, and apart from the odd tramlines in his uniform trousers my ironing was pretty much up to scratch as well. As for the rest, well I shall have to leave you guessing.

Equally well I can recall testing him on the Theft Act 1968 – section 10(1) 'Aggravated Burglary' to be exact – which states that an offence has been committed where a burglar enters a building and 'at the time has with him a Weapon of offence, Imitation firearm, Firearm or any Explosives.' In other words he has taken his WIFE with him on the job. The question of whether or not the burglar actually used the weapon would not be up for debate; the point being that he or she had entered the premises with something that had the potential to cause harm.

Equally the point is that whilst the word WIFE is spelt in the same way as a marital title, in the context of my scenario the meanings could not be further apart. One could not possibly liken one to the other, or 'misdiagnose' the intention within the act of stealing.

Mnemonics are also common place in nursing. The word NEWS stands for National Early Warning Score. It is part of a charting system. It is intended to detect the degree of a person's illness and prompt critical care intervention so that the medical team can try to identify the cause and address it accordingly. Used in hospital wards, it covers six vital parameters – a person's pulse, blood pressure, temperature, respiratory rate, mental state and oxygen saturation levels, and it is the ideal way to determine the presence and severity of a person's illness and especially where sepsis may be suspected.

Serum lactate levels in the blood have been hailed as a surrogate marker for tissue perfusion, and unless sustained within satisfactory limits a person's vital organs can start to shut down. The rule of thumb is that the more elevated the lactate is, the higher the mortality rate – it is a key element in how sepsis, septic shock or other trauma such as internal bleeding is managed. Typically, where a person's result is above normal levels after an initial evaluation, treatment should be initiated without delay if they are to have any chance of a successful recovery. The choice of antibiotics within the first few hours is crucial and a patient's history of drinking or smoking, for want of an example, should not deter the clinicians from considering other potential sources of infection that may account for the scores that arise from this type of recording.

So I have explained what 'aggravated burglary' is. The punishment of that crime involves four elements – the use of weapons, the status of the victim, the intent of the perpetrator and the degree of injury caused. So why is it that there is no such crime as 'Aggravated Death' or 'Death by Aggravation'? Should those who act with reckless indifference to human life not also be punished? Why should injections, medication or medical apparatus not be considered potential 'weapons?' Is not giving someone an under-dose or overdose or too much or too little oxygen an 'assault' on a patient's well-being – their central nervous system – for example? These things may have made matters worse – increased the intensity of the patient's symptoms to such a degree that the end result is so severe it cannot be undone. Where such instruments cause harm time and time again, why are they not considered to be weapons in the same way as a firearm or an explosive, and why should the clinicians not be punished in the same way as a burglar or murderer might be? Should it matter any less where patients come from or how they have chosen to live their lives?

'Perpetrator' might be too strong a word to use in this scenario, as I really am not suggesting for one minute that any of the 'persons of interest' set out to intentionally cause harm. They were not evil, but there were certain aspects within the pathway of care that could be deemed unlawful in terms of breaches in government legislation which is laid down in law and the illegal aspect of altering legal documents to get themselves out of a sticky situation.

As for the degree of injury caused, how could it be more severe than death? And is an incorrect interpretation of a clinical tool that results in unnecessary harm not as harmful as a firearm?

Yet unless you are in the privileged position of being able to afford a top-notch solicitor, despite having evidence for breaches in duty of care and how harm could have been avoided, you have to, as they sat, 'put up or shut up.' It is this that in my mind is criminal.

Woah! How heavy is this getting, I can here you say, but have I not every right to be suspicious over the completion of a nursing chart/observational tool that is largely based on subjective matter?

So you might liken me to Red Rum on speed, but I am betting that you will be able to see the crossover between clinical and criminal law. Forgive me. I hope you are not aggravated by this!

Before we adjourn and head to the pub for a few swift halves, giving any smokers among you the chance to puff on a 'vape', 'rollie' or pre-prepared fag to prepare you for the long nutty road ahead, can you please humour me in a little google-woogling while you are out there? You will? Great!

First check out the side effects of co-codamol 30/500mgs and tramadol 50mgs on someone with anything from mild to severe liver disease, whether alcohol-related or not. Here, this will help you: https://bnf.org.uk. Next look up the 'normal' ranges for a person's (a) white blood cell count, (b) creatinine level, (c) alkaline phosphatase level, (d) c-reactive protein level, (d) glucose level and (e) lactate level so you will be better equipped to understand the six sepsis markers and where they all fit in.

As the story unfolds you will learn how the Coroner had limited the inquest to the 'who', the 'what' and the 'where' of how hubby died. It is my intention to leave no stone unturned in *my* WHOdunnit, HOWdunnit, WHEREdunnit and WHATdunnit scenario which may open up a bigger can of worms.

I need to make a few important phone calls before

we start, and if I can be permitted to say to you all in true Columbo fashion, 'Oh and there is just one more thing', don't forget to stub your fags out in the right ashtray.

Let's say we meet back here in 40 shakes of a widow's tale.

The boy

The young PC

Inspector first class

Happy-go-lucky Hubby

I keep clicking my heels three times, but it doesn't bring you back

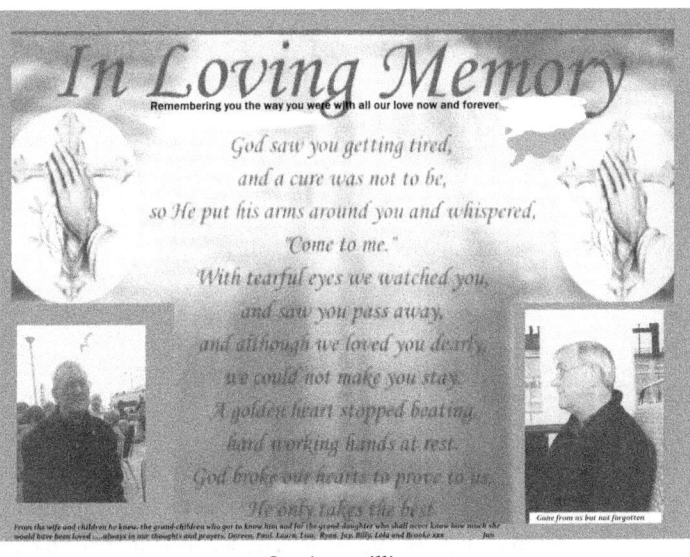

One in a million

# WHAT'S APP DOC?

Since I am renowned for turning sad fact into comical fiction, and in a bid to try to get my message across in a non-depressive way, my first thought was to approach Rumpole of the Old Bailey. However, I remember someone warning me that he always defended and never prosecuted, even in the most criminal of cases – he was more intent on winning the popularity stakes, especially among the middle and upper class breed of 'criminal', instead of bringing them to justice.

A consultant's wage in comparison to the meagre amount I earn as a bog-standard nurse then would have them win the case before it had already started, so perhaps I shall pass on this one. OK, so we do not have the electric chair in this country (thank God) and whilst it is not my intention that any of the clinicians who I maintain let hubby down should be banged up in a condemned Victorian slum, living in cooped up conditions with psychopaths and having to fight for the use of the one and only chamber pot, they do need to take responsibility for that which they wrongly did or failed to do.

I am not in the market for dating, but should I be, then I might think (speech bubbles) 'Who needs Tinder when there is Rinder?' And yes, I am fully aware that even if I were literally the last woman on this earth I still would not be his type. What a striking looking man, however – always cheerful and grinning like a Cheshire cat – perhaps I could borrow him as a prop for my proposed winter Mad Hatter tea party bash come December.

So I am being idiotic, but the law can be a right ass sometimes, can't it? I mean, 'men's rear' appears to mean a bunch of legal guys talking out of their backsides, does it not, or am I just guilty of spelling it wrong? Trust me – it was deliberate!

OK, so Robbie boy may not be a real judge, but he *is* a real criminal barrister and leave aside his charismatic charm he may be the only one who could appreciate my wit, summarise my case wearing his night-cap, oops I mean over a night cap, and be able to deduce the real issues that are open to speculation and point me in the right direction. I have summoned his help via the ITV Hub – I have two hopes he will turn up – some hope and Bob Hope.

For all my mouthing off I am really a shy girl – why do you think I am called Brooke? Because I am like a gentle running stream, that's why.

I really do not relish the thought of having to stand up in front of everyone in my fictitious court and quiz the suspects, and if I start to go to pieces then Robbie will not take me seriously and the buggers will get away with it again. My cousin on the other hand is more 'Niagara Falls' – more forthright – and his own unique style of questioning will flow so much better than I could ever hope to achieve. His name is not Vinny by the way, but he has picked up a few tips of his along the way (having been compelled to watch the film no less than five times). Nevertheless, in order to protect Dave's real identity I shall use this as his 'prosecuting' name.

I have sent him an SOS message on WhatsApp. I shall know whether he has read it or not!

While you have been sloshing and puffing away I have been looking for a 'pop up' courtroom on ebay, but sadly I have had no luck. I had one slot left in an unpackaged four-roomed dolls' house in which I had considered recreating the Old Bailey, but still there is no one to drag it in from the garage for me. So the best I have been able to rustle up is a tent similar to that used in the 'Great British Bake Off' with a small gazebo erected at the side to act as a witness box. Well, I did warn you that there would be no 'credible' environment in which to lay out my case. Whilst it may not have any extra features like a dance floor, it is of a good quality, good lighting and is spotless, and it is just right to create the unique atmosphere that I seek to portray here today. It had one previous owner and I managed to snipe someone for it at £19.99 – bargain!

If only I had a proper office, I was thinking, in which to hold the 'trial,' I might be able to keep a tape recorder under my desk and hide a microphone from view behind a flower pot.

If you are not already one step ahead of me then I should explain to the rest of my jurors that one's larynx is like an instrument and as with DNA everyone's vocal chords are different, so if anyone were to turn up today trying to pretend to be someone else then I would have been able to catch them red handed, but I don't, so I can't!

If it were footprints I was after, I might also accidentally on purpose knock over a whole heap of sherbet onto the floor to covertly get an impression of the culprit's size nines or otherwise that I could dust around afterwards. However, I am not sure this would be admissible in a court of law, and besides it is their fingerprints I am more interested in.

Why, you ask? Because within that 'hiding place' where the important 'persons of interest' all wear white coats and have the same lanyards and similar stethoscopes around their necks, there is little to distinguish one from the other, yet the probability of finding a sufficiently similar fingerprint in my 'target' population is very small.

As the flap on the tent flaps widely open before the West Country wind, with diamond-studded gravel in hand, wearing a black glittery robe made from Lurex, and donning a sparkly emerald green perruque, this chap waltzes in announcing it is 'bob-a-job' week. Well, his name *is* Bob – let's hope he is up to the job! But wait, he looks like Robbie in some ways, but there is something not quite right about him. He tells me he is Robbie's twin brother Gilbert but everyone calls him Gobbie because he has a right mouth on him. Not like his sibling then, I am thinking, who, though riddled with sarcasm, is by all accounts quite demure. This could indeed be interesting, I am thinking, as Gilbert sets to imitate his bro.'

So here you all are seated behind the pages of my book and there sits Gobbie at the head of Paul Hollywood's cake-judging table, suited' and with laptop booted. He plans to type up the events on it as they unfold. Stenographers, I am told, are now a thing of the past. Gobbie had better take this seriously – I don't want to find that he has instead been using the laptop to suss out how to cook Mary Berry's favourite apple pie.

I am finding it hard not to point the finger at the 'suspects' as they enter the tent one by one to the sound of Blue on the speakers dotted around the PVC covering, as I hum away to myself, 'You're the ones with the money and the free ride' (litigation authority). 'You're here 'cos of the lies that you all denied'.

'All rise' Gobbie said. 'All rise.'

In smirk mode, I was thinking that soon they

would 'be on the stand with their backs against the wall, nowhere to run and nobody they could call/I just couldn't wait now my case was opened wide, they would need to pray, but my jurors (that's you lot remember) will decide' (Blue 2001).

In a bid to get close enough to try to establish what wonderful aftershave he was wearing after he had pirouetted into the tent, I was seizing the opportunity to whisper in Gobbie's ear, 'Your honour please, gotta believe what I say, what I will have my cousin tell, happened not the other day but many moons ago.'

I went on 'I must confess that I've had about enough and I swear I will get my cousin to tell the truth about all the things they did do and how they thought they had me fooled and if you have an ounce of sympathy in that slender-toned body of yours then any objections must be overruled.'

In my experience a Double Diamond is not the only thing that 'works wonders' – so does a bit of flattery here and there.

Just need to check my mobile and see if ... no wait, panic over my 'cuzzy-wuzzy' has arrived. He tells me his head is feeling a bit fuzzy-fuzzy where he has been bending down all day helping out on the plantation at Tara, yet he managed to get here from Twelve Oaks in record time, just in time for the 'hearing.'

This is where I stand back and let Gobbie and 'Vinny' take over the proceedings that the suspects might get rumbled.

Gobbie: 'Calling the first two suspects from the Make-Me-Wait Medical Centre - Doctor Abacus (one) and Doctor Abacus (two). Before you answer any questions, you need to be sworn in.'

As they stand in front of him, one in a pea-green suit, the other in heavily-creased khaki Oxford bags, Gobbie asks them to take the BNF jointly in their hands and repeat after him the conventional 'We swear to tell the truth the whole truth and nothing but the truth.'

Harmoniously Dr AB1 and Dr AB2 blurt out, 'I swear to tell the truth, the whole truth, and whatever.'

Vinny then asks them to sign the attendance register.

Vinny: 'Between ** and ** did you both work at the Make-Me-Wait Medical Centre and did you each prescribe to your patient strong painkillers for lower back pain?' Vinny was trying to confirm they had worked at that GP practice at that time before they could come up with an alibi.

Dr AB1 and Dr AB2 (one after the other) 'Yes I did on both counts.'

Vinny: ' Are you both aware that good medical practice as a GP means that you must maintain and develop your knowledge and skills in pharmacology and therapeutics, as well as prescribing and medicines management, relevant to your role and prescribing practice?

'I am' replies Dr AB1, whose ears resemble the handles of the FA cup trophy that Vinny tried not to focus too much on in order to keep a straight face.

'I am,' says Dr AB2, whose ears are more rounded, giving him more of a resemblance to Mickey Mouse.

Vinny: 'Are you familiar with the guidance in the British National Formulary (BNF) which contains essential information to help you prescribe, monitor, supply, and administer medicines?'

Dr AB1 and Dr AB2 (in harmony) 'I am.'

Vinny: 'Does the General Medical Council under which you operate not also state that a doctor should prescribe only where necessary and consider the benefits versus the risks? And does it not also state that a GP must take note of a patient's medical history (and especially any liver or kidney problems) as well as any concurrent medications before prescribing? Furthermore, does it not also state that a GP should think about doses carefully and not work on the notion that 'one dose fits all?'

Dr AB1 and Dr AB2 (arguably annoyed), 'Yes on both accounts, but I am sure I took everything into account.'

Vinny: 'Are you sure? I don't think so.'

Vinny: 'If so, then why Dr AB1 did you, in the first instance, prescribe to your patient the drug Co-codamol at the highest strength of 30/500 mgs, two four times daily, when a lower dose would have been more appropriate and might have sufficed? Could it have been that as a stand-in for his own GP you were not fully aware of his medical history and if not, why not, as could that not have led to such inappropriate prescribing? Were there no other alternatives that would have sought to be gentler on the liver?'

Dr AB1 looks quite flustered but makes no comment.

'Dr AB2,' says Vinny, directing his gaze at his partner, 'as the patient's regular GP, were you even aware that your colleague had prescribed the above painkillers before you yourself, having then prescribed Tramadol, albeit in the only dose available, 50 mgs, gave instructions for Mr T to take 100mgs four times daily as needed? If not, why not? Is it not good practice that where you had been away you should have checked your patient's medication history to make sure there was no overlap of treatment that could cause harm? And where your patient was confronted with two sets of painkillers, was it not important for him to know whether or not one should cancel out the other at the risk of taking them sequentially?'

Neither GP comments at this stage, instead looking very uncomfortable and confused.

'I put it to you, Your Judgeship' Vinny says, turning to Gobbie, 'that neither Dr AB1 nor Dr AB2 *had* considered the side effects of either of those medications, which should have been avoided, or at least been given at reduced doses to someone with a history of drinking/liver disease.

'Dr AB2, as Ted's regular GP, should have seen where they was an overlap in treatment that had the potential for dose-related toxicity which in turn could lead to kidney problems, let alone the more common side effects of hypotension and respiratory depression as a result of large doses of these very strong painkillers, difficulty urinating, nausea and dizziness, and in the worst case scenario, the risk of going into a coma.'

'It is my opinion, Your Judgeship, that both GP's cocked up on all accounts and that they did not consider the risks over the benefit. That they should have refrained from prescribing each of these drugs given Ted's medical history, should have ensured that he was aware that he should not take them both at the same time, at the risk of causing aggravation to his liver.'

Vinny: 'What do you have to say for yourselves, doctors? '

Both doctors shrug their shoulders.

'No more questions.'

Gobbie (to Dr AB1 and Dr AB2): 'Leave the gazebo and go and sit near the biscuit-judging table for the time being.'

If only 'Painless Peter Potter' were a real person, I was thinking, Ted might have been in safer hands. All he really needed was a bit of laughing gas to take his mind off his back pain (*The Paleface,* 1948).

I whisper in Vinny's ear: 'Get the lollipop kid up next.'

'I want to call the lollipop kid to the stand next, Your Judgeship,' Vinny says to Gobbie, seeking reassurance that it is OK. I did not expect Vinny to blurt it out in this way and as everyone looks around the tented 'courtroom' in wonder that no one had actually come forward, I realises he had made an embarrassing boo-boo.

Me (Brooke) to Vinny (with cupped hand over his left lughole): 'That's not his real name. I should have told you that, I am sorry.'

Incidentally, if you are wondering why I refer to Doc AB3 as the lollipop kid, it is for no other reason that he is short and dumpy, although his dress sense is marginally better than the Munchkin midgets.

'Calling Doctor Abacus (three) to the witness stand,' shouts Vinny once the embarrassment has worn off. Handing him a hardback version of *The Wizard of Oz,* Vinny asks Dr AB3 to place his hand on it and explain why he is here today. In a squeaky voice he begins to sing:

'I represent the medical kids,
The medical kids,
The medical kids,
I represent the medical kids
And welcome you to GP land.'

Gobbie cannot resist doing a 'Strictly' dance impression of a Munchkin, racing back to the cake judging table, I mean the 'bar', before the Doc has finished.

'Ok, right. Thanks for that Gobbo,' says Vinny, in awe of his fellow court mate, 'but we really must get on.'

I guess a tent with a dance floor might have come in handy, after all I am thinking at this moment.

'Do you solemnly swear to tell the truth, the whole truth and whatever, er, I mean nothing but the truth, so help you God'? Vinny asks of the innocent-looking lad.

'I do' replies Dr AB3, the one who, with his chubby

face and wide forehead, truly lives up to his nickname.

Vinny then asks the doc to sign the attendance register. Vinny: 'When Ted walked into your surgery on ** of ** how would you have described him?'

Dr AB3: 'He looked pale, quite anaemic and was quite dizzy.'

Vinny: 'What did you do next?'

Dr AB3: 'I checked his blood pressure, listened to his chest, and listened to what Ted had to say. He told me he was concerned about some blood loss from 'down below' and that he had been feeling nauseous, had lost his appetite, had been peeing less and felt breathless, which was unusual for him, even as a smoker.'

Vinny: 'Did you at any time discuss his back pain, or were you aware of any medication that he had been taking other than what you printed out from your computer as his non-regular GP?'

Dr AB3 was unable to recall any such conversation or what steps he had taken to check Ted's recent medication history.

Vinny: 'What were your first thoughts on this man's condition, doc?'

Doc AB3: 'I had a brief understanding of Ted's drinking habit and of the fact that he had smoked for a good number of years, so I carried out a few eliminatory checks. I listened to his chest – there were a few 'crackles' – I thought he might have a chest infection brewing; I checked for yellowing in his eyes and on his skin as jaundice can indicate a serious problem with the liver, for one thing. Ted's skin was very pale, not even a hint of magnolia, let alone a yellow tinge. I had come to recognise the signs of liver failure, as most of my patients would come to me looking like Homer Simpson and ask me if they could have one last Duff beer before they meet their maker. This man did not fit the criteria'.

At that point Vinny was warming to the doc, as he liked his sense of humour even if it was a little insensitive and maybe a little unethical when it came to stereotyping, yet urged him to continue.

'I then checked his fingers for what we call digital 'clubbing' as it is a common finding in someone who has serious problems with their liver. Ted's fingers were normal,' he replied, adding that Ted had told him the last time he had gone clubbing was in 1976 when he had taken his bride-to-be to Annabella's nightclub in Golders Green.

Vinny: 'So what were you thinking, doc?'

Doc AB3: 'I wasn't really sure, because in most drinkers when they get to the point where there are complications with their liver they will end up with a huge 'belly' which accumulates fluid, infected fluid usually. There might be noticeable blood loss in their stools, but this can also be as the result of a burst ulcer, so not necessarily anything sinister.'

Vinny: 'So what are you saying, doc?'

Doc AB3: 'That since Ted was of a slight built and quite proud of his figure, given his age, yet looked so pale, and had a seriously low blood pressure reading, and since he had passed all the eliminatory checks, I was thinking that perhaps this was the case, as it would have explained his symptoms.'

Vinny: 'So what did you do?'

Doc AB3: 'I asked his missus to drive him to Firchester Hospital nearby. I printed off a summary of his medical history, which included what medication he was on, and I wrote my findings and concerns in pen at the bottom. I gave this to Ted in a sealed envelope and asked him to give it to the receptionist when he arrived. This is the usual process with referrals.'

Vinny: 'Were you aware that the medication list you printed out was not up-to-date and did not include the prescribed painkillers? Having carried out your own checks, did you feel it was appropriate for you to disclose to the hospital details about the man's visits over the previous months which had no bearing on what was going on at that point in time, and that your handwritten addition should have been enough?'

'No, and I did not give it a second thought,' the doc replied, trying to answer the points put to him.

Vinny: 'Was Ted of sound body and mind when he came to you? Could he not have answered any questions that were put to him by hospital staff about his present and past medical condition which would have prevented the unlawful disclosure since he had opted out of sharing such information with anyone outside of the surgery a good nine months previously ,and that which was clearly recorded on the system the day he came to you?'

'Yes he was. Yes he could have done. I didn't think about that,' replied Doc AB3 sequentially, then tried to justify himself on the latter by saying that he did not have time to read the criteria about summary use and had just printed it off automatically, as he was keen for Mr T to go to the Firchester as quickly as possible.'

Vinny: 'Is it possible that the way Ted presented to you on the * day of * 20** could have been consistent with drug-induced liver injury, and that had you checked your own records thoroughly and known about those two painkillers that he had been taking you might have included this as a relative link?'

Doc AB3: 'It's not for me to speculate. I don't know – perhaps.'

Vinny: 'Could it be that Mr T had been overdosing on these tablets without his knowledge, and they would have festered in his system over a number of weeks, causing his blood to become poisoned, which in fact is what the term sepsis means? Isn't that right doctor?'

'I say this' said Vinny. 'The Coroner had told Ted's wife that there was no evidence of liver failure so, in your opinion doc, is it likely that it was instead his kidneys that had started to fail, leading to problems with his heart which resulted in him going into respiratory arrest?'

At that point Doc AB3 did not know what to say.

'So you have nothing to say doctor, any more than your colleagues, and you wonder why I have referred to you each in turn as Doctor Abacus, which, for the record, is because I was already made aware that nothing you would say would add up.' he made a point of saying this in front of the 'Judge.'

It is at this point I am wondering if the 'Hi 5' response between Gobbie and Vinny is really appropriate under such serious circumstances or indeed very professional; they met in the middle of the room to slap palms before getting the doc to 'stand down'.

Before we carry on, have you worked out yet my clever tactic to get evidence 'covertly' that I can link to the 'persons of interest' in the scheme of things?

Yes, that's right – in getting each suspect to swear on a different book which has been treated with invisible black metallic fingerprinting powder and in getting them to sign an attendance record that can later be matched up against Mr T's medical notes I will be able to confirm who wrote them, who might have altered them and who had actually signed them, with the suspects being none the wiser. Fingerprints, you see, are one of the few types of evidence that cannot be bluffed. Am I clever or am I clever?

Gobbie has just whispered in my ear that he needs to make a phone call to a good friend of his who ran away to join a travelling circus, so he wants another recess. These endless breaks are all well and good, I am thinking, but the sooner we get this sorry matter wrapped up the sooner I can go home to knock myself up a vindaloo and catch up on my Z Cars box set. I am extremely hungry. What is the point of hanging around a cake-baking tent without making full use of the facilities? What say you jurors, that you each head out to your own kitchens and knock up a cake for yourselves to munch away at as you continue to indulge me in my tales of woe? I shall get Paul (you know, the one with the piercing blue eyes) and Mary to judge them. Email the pictures across and they can make their minds up as to what they might taste like in order to extract a winner.

This 'trial' so far has definitely given me culinary inspiration. I shall opt for a *croque en bouche* I think, on account of the cock and bull stories I have heard so far today. That has to be a winner surely!

Twenty minutes later. Luckily I have just finished putting the finishing touches to my 'pile of profiteroles' (which in essence is all it is, in much the same way as oeufs en cocotte just means eggs in a pot). Gobbie now wants to hear a little more about how Ted had come to meet the 'dumpy kid' in the first place so he could put things into perspective. Care to share? OK, listen up!

# FIFTY SHADES OF INNOCENCE

Ted rarely went to the doctor's, I told Gobbie, except when he needed a new medication prescription or the GP needed to update him on any blood results.

It was our last night of cruising around the tropical islands on a much-anticipated holiday, and we had booked ourselves a place in the most exclusive of the ship's restaurants to finish off a truly remarkable fortnight. Ted, however, had to make his excuses on a couple of occasions as he raced off to the gentleman's 'powder room', having felt quite nauseous, leaving me sitting there alone at the table all dressed up to the nines, the attendants assuming we had had some kind of row.

The meal was cut short at the dessert stage, because all Ted wanted to do was to go back to our cabin and sleep. As I sat alone on the balcony glancing over towards him I was thinking that this was not how we had planned to spend the last night of what had been a premature wedding anniversary treat to ourselves. It was not his fault. I did not blame him.

As each marital year passed hubby would say the same thing to me, whether it was after the 32nd, 33rd or 34th year – 'God girl, if I had committed murder I would be out by now.'

This year was no exception, although he did not quite feel up to joking. Surprisingly enough he had drunk very little on our holiday and eaten less – both quite out of character. I knew him better than anyone, and I knew how resilient he had been against the effects of drinking and smoking over the years. On this particular holiday, where he had eaten and drunk far less than expected, something was penetrating his armour, yet we were unable at that time to pin-point what it might have been. The ship's doctor put it down to dehydration after Ted temporarily passed out on the deck a few hours before we were due to go for that meal. The temperatures had been extremely high over the two weeks and Ted's tolerance to the heat was in no way as hardy as mine. However, a bag of fluids given subcutaneously soon put him right, or so it seemed at the time.

The relief of arriving back on dry land once we hit Port Lauderdale could not be under-estimated, yet when hubby came over all not-so-funny later that evening in Johnny Rockets our concerns escalated. I will be forever indebted to an American stranger who insisted on dropping us back at our luxury hotel when I had no way of getting hold of a yellow cab.

We landed back at Gatwick Airport in the early hours of the following morning. We had booked a hotel for the night before we had left England, as Ted did not relish the thought of tackling the M25 at rush hour, and we used that day to visit the place where we had first lived as man and wife – the free police house that came with the job as a new member of the Surrey Constabulary. As he left for work each morning dressed in his powder blue shirt brushed up against a black jacket with its polished silver buttons and immaculately-pressed black trousers, I was filled with immense pride in my new hubby. However, less than two weeks after we had wed I thought I was going to be a widow, after an incident with colliding cars and flying debris as he was controlling the traffic during the annual London to Brighton veteran car rally. Fortunately for me, he escaped with little more than bruised legs and a broken finger, else my life could have taken a whole new path. The *Crawley and District Observer* even wanted a picture of us on our wedding day – our only experience of making the limelight.

It was more poignant therefore that I insisted that Ted should let me take a photograph of him on this particular day, standing outside that very same police station, his first post, almost 35 years on, although he was in civvies this time. He hated having his picture taken, but he indulged me, not imagining for one minute that it was to be the last picture I would ever take of him.

He managed to get us home safely the following morning, even though he was still not feeling one hundred percent well. Having already promised to play tour guide for a family member prior to our recent trip, as it approached I had not realised that Ted had gone back to his GP to ask for more painkillers, aware that his back pain might flare up again once he had to spend time seeking out the local tourist attractions of the Nile cruise.

Now on that trip, neither the kids nor I could get hold of Ted on his mobile to wish him happy birthday. I amusedly picturing him sitting cross-legged on the sands of the desert with flute in hand trying to conjure up Catherine Zeta-Jones from a wicker basket – his 'darling bud of September' (*Road to Bali,* 1952), so our emotions were a mixture of hoping he was having a good time and annoyance that he might think we had forgotten his special day.

The following morning, in an apologetic voice, Ted confessed that the day's hiking had taken a toll on him, that he had again felt unwell and had just wanted to sleep, even missing a birthday meal that had been planned for him by his travelling companion.

Whilst now home safely yet again, hubby appeared quite pale and weak, as if all the stuffing had been knocked out of him, and I was adamant that he should go back to his doctor without any unnecessary delay. He left it to me, the insistent wife, to book an urgent appointment first thing the following morning once the surgery opened.

'Hurry up or we'll be late!' I called up to Ted from the hallway as he was faffing around as he always did after having a bath. 'Won't be a minute love' he shouted down.

'Come on grandad', I could hear our three-year-old grandson mutter, having raced upstairs to find Ted sitting on the bed in what we refer to as the 'Andy Pandy' room. Weird as this may sound, please rest assured that it is not decorated with cable ties, nor anything held up with duck tape. The stuffed blue and white striped 'dolls' that I picked up at a car boot sale, *not* a hardware store, hardly evoke an erotic response. It's just that the only thing I am fixated on is collecting childhood memorabilia to pass down to the grandkids. The only things in the house that are remotely *Fifty Shades of Grey* are hubby's old artist's pencils and charcoals by Winsor and Newton which come in various lengths (what is it that they say in the man's world – small, medium and liar?) so 'draw' from that what you will, just don't 'paint' a bad picture of me. I have my nurse's rep to protect! I am innocent by disassociation with anything remotely risqué. There is no dark side to me; those dolls are not 'objects of my desire', and I could quite easily bin them tomorrow if I wanted to, so thanks but no thanks Mr Freud, that blows your psychoanalytical theory out the window somewhat, doesn't it?

As his lordship followed the gentle child down the stairs, his dizziness was quite apparent. Don't get me wrong, my wifely duties had no bounds, but considering hubby had spent several decades running defence establishments it was a bit of a fall from grace, him having to get me, the missus, to help tie his shoe laces, so we could head off to the quack's before we got slapped with a £20 fine for being late for our appointment. He was too out of breath to do it himself.

'You'll have me wiping your backside next' I laughed, having joked over the years that this was probably the one and only thing that I had managed to avoid in our lifetime together. Neither of us were saints. We had had our ups and downs and yet had come through some very trying times with a lot of heartache along the way, because no matter what life threw at us we were in it together for the long-haul. It was always us against the world.

Ted's pride prevented him from holding onto my arm as we walked towards my car, parked across the road of our little cul-de-sac. Luckily the surgery was no more than a stone's throw away.

When they called his name, the nipper and I waited outside, but it was not long before we were called in, and that is where the lollipop kid came in.

Gobbie: 'Well thank you my dear – I bet you thought I wouldn't give a damn – but quite frankly I do, and I hope others sitting in judgement today would also have lent a sympathetic ear.

# MISSING THE POINT

———◦∞◦———

Mae West is reported to have said, 'it is better to be looked over than overlooked.' She meant herself, of course, but in my game of who/what/when/howdunnit I do not want you good people to overlook even the smallest detail, and whilst it is a serious subject that brings me here today, hopefully my subtle use of humour is helping to ease the tension at your end as my writing is definitely providing me with a little respite from the difficult moments that continue to lie ahead.

Sheepishly appearing from around the back of the tent, the clinicians take their places in the witness box as Gobbie calls them in. Whilst there had been many fingers in Ted's clinical pie, it was these three that had been selectively chosen by their manager to represent the Firchester. Huddled together within the confines of the small gazebo they are sworn in one by one, each in turn placing his hands on the 20th edition of *Gray's Anatomy* (1918 edition).

'We swear to tell the truth, the whole truth and whatever,' they say, each keeping one hand behind his back with fingers crossed. As Vinny prepares to question the clinicians he denies them any access to Ted's medical notes, but again ensures the attendance register had been signed by each of them.

He was trying to establish at this stage two things. First of all, could they actually recall what their patient looked like, and secondly did they understand what the terms *missed diagnosis and misdiagnosis* meant. He also wanted to learn if they knew the difference between a *diagnosis* and a *differential diagnosis*.

Have you heard the one about the Irishman who is asked to take part in an identity parade after a woman has accused someone of attacking her? Before she even gets half way along the line, the Irishman steps forward, points at the lady and cries 'that's the one!' It's a very old joke, I know, but I was thinking if only things were that simple. If only any one of the clinicians might remember Ted and the events as they had occurred, then there might actually be a pricking of conscience and one of them, if not all, might actually step forward and own up to what went wrong.

If only I had thought to create an identi-flip book like the ones I used to enjoy as a kid when trying to make up different characters from a series of overlapping sections of a page I might at least have been able to jog their memories, but it is too late now.

As you seek to decide whether or not any of the suspects had come up to professional scratch, let me try and help you, because there are so many different things that come under the umbrella term of 'diagnosis', whether the cause of a person's illness is as the result of a medical, clinical or physical problem. Where clinicians rely only on patient 'interview' and what they have been able to establish from their medical records, allowing it to take precedence over physical examination, observed signs and symptoms, laboratory tests, or basic gut instinct this is where the danger of a wrong diagnosis may arise.

A 'differential diagnosis' is where a patient might have several diseases and it needs to be determined which of those in particular might be responsible for the symptoms that prevail. A 'missed diagnosis' is the term given when a doctor fails to identify a potential medical condition that has been posed to them and do not carry out any diagnostic test to confirm or deny it. A 'misdiagnosis' is when a doctor has diagnosed a person with the wrong condition. Basically one can stem from another, yet it is a clever play on words and quite easily one can get away with murder.

I on the other hand do not mince my words. Naïve I may be, but a cock-up is still a cock-up.

'Do you each confirm that you are registered with

the General Medical Council – the GMC'? Vinny asked the medics one by one, looking them straight in the eye. Seeing that Gobbie looked a little puzzled, Vinny took a minute to explain to him that this was a regulatory body that oversees good medical practice and the contract by which clinicians are bound.

'We do' replied the clinicians in sync.

Vinny: 'Are your chief responsibilities therefore not to 'protect, promote and maintain the health and safety of the public', and are you equally aware that you risk facing being suspended or struck off the register if at any time you fail to uphold that which it seeks to promote?'

Nonchalantly they replied 'Yes.'

'I don't like your tone of voice', replied Gobbie. 'They smell a funny colour.'

'Any more of this attitude and I shall hold you in contempt of court, do you understand, you poxymorons?'

Forcing a smile so hard that it looked as if he had been acutely injected with Botox, Gobbie turned towards the one with the handlebars for a moustache, who confirmed they would toe the line from now on.

Vinny laid out the criteria for deductive reasoning versus diagnostic unreasonableness.

'It is my understanding' began Vinny, 'that a *clinical* diagnosis is that which should be based on a person's signs, symptoms and laboratory findings, whereas a *medical* diagnosis is based upon how a person presents, to a GP for example, of the regularity or irregularity of the person's heartbeat, of any unusual sounds that have been detected either in the stomach or lungs through external examination, or in relation to any unusual sounds that a GP or other clinician might pick up through a stethoscope in which circulatory, respiratory or even bowel concerns can be detected. Is my understanding correct?' Vinny asked of them. They proceeded to nod in unison.

'Had Mr T's GP - Doc AB3 to you - not already done the preliminary checks regards inspection, palpitation, percussion and auscultation, eliminating an automatic diagnosis but instead considering then that the only explanation for conflicting 'results' might be due to internal bleeding for which the gentleman was forwarded to you in the first place?' Gobbie jumped in, glaring at the three stooges for an answer. 'And was it not the case,' Gobbie continued, 'that in spite of this nothing was *actually* done about the GP's presumptive diagnosis?

'I understand that one of you, or maybe a colleague who is not here today, had written in this chap's notes that he had sepsis,' Gobbie went on, now on a roll, 'but that this was then crossed off by another of you people and replaced with 'alcohol liver disease', even though he had presented with at least three of the symptoms indicative of a life-threatening illness such as hypothermia, an increased respiratory rate and low urinary output, for which a catheter was inserted to monitor his progress in this particular direction.

'I am also aware that this man then ended up on the High-Dependency Unit a few hours later because of problems that related particularly to this low blood pressure reading. I gather bloods had been taken and despite his lactate level, his creatinine level and especially his C-reactive protein level, which alone was raised to over 50 times the normal level, no one appeared to be fazed by this. Who among you had taken the decision to alter the preliminary diagnosis based only on third-hand information that should have had no bearing on the critical vital signs of a severe infection?'

Gobbie's hackles were now well and truly up. All three docs looked at each other, hoping someone would make the first move commentary wise yet no one dared to utter a word.

If nothing else, Robbie had told Gobbie that it took more than legal knowledge for a barrister to be able to sit in judgement on a case. He should pay particular attention to the body language of 'persons of interest', as it could be a good way to tell if they were lying or partially lying, but none of them were giving anything away.

Scanning them one by one, Gobbie was wondering what they had to hide; the five foot nine middle-aged gentleman with the pasty freckled skin, the one with the chocolate brown eyes who, whilst a good deal shorter, resembled Precious McKenzie in stature, and the one with the devilishly good looks who exceeded the six-foot mark with dark curly locks and eyes the colour of blue curaçao, who he knew would be right up his brother's street had it not been for the fact that he was already spoken for. Besides, thought Gobbie, curaçao is naturally colourless, so perhaps this particular 'person of interest' didn't actually have a lot up top, as it were.

Since he had observed a lack of any response from them to his questioning so far, Gobbie knew he had to up his game by continuing to fire questions at them that might eventually break through their guarded and restrictive personae in the hope that they might retaliate and reveal inconsistencies between what they had told the Coroner at the inquest and what they were telling him now.

The judge stated: 'Having had a chance to consider Mr T's blood results during the time of his admission, and more importantly in the hours leading up to his death, do you deny:

'That between day one and day six Ted's white blood cell count (white blood cells being those that help fight infection) had been raised beyond normal levels and that this had trebled by the time he died?

'That on the day of his admission Ted's creatinine level – a blood test that seeks to identify any problems with a person's kidneys – was double the highest level of normality, yet all you sought to do in his case was to shove a catheter in at the risk of introducing more infection? Surely any medic with an ounce of common sense would know that a person's kidneys are one of the first organs to be affected when someone has sepsis,' Gobbie said, then handed the questioning back to Vinny.

'Was it not the case,' proceeded Vinny, 'that on the day of Mr T's admission, despite his initial blood result in relation to the alkaline phosphate level being raised, instead of considering for one minute that it could have been as a result of say, undiagnosed cancer or drug-induced hepatitis, you automatically assumed that it was because of advanced liver damage as a result of his long-term drinking, and you amended his medical notes to this effect? Furthermore, is it not also the case that because Mr T's gamma-glutamyl transferase level was also raised, that which is more often than not linked to alcohol liver disease, in putting together the raised GGT level, you were so blinkered in your assessment that you failed to consider any connection between this and drug induced toxicity?'

The room was silent but for the sound of the refrigerator fans whirling in the background. Aware that he had pinned the doc into a corner, Vinny felt enough had been said, enough for the jurors to work with, thinking that what had promised to be an amusing take on a game of Cluedo was turning out to be a right old legal thriller.

OK, so the docs had not performed badly, but I forbid you to boo them or throw any rotten cakes at them as they now leave the tent. It is something I myself consider to be very rude, and besides they have not been condemned yet, so dignity please, ladies and gentlemen.

# A RIGHT CARRY ON

—◦◦◦—

All this is enough to drive anyone to drink, isn't it, I say, staring at the 'there's always time for a glass of wine' plaque hanging up here in my dining room, but I actually fancy a drop of Blue Nun right now, so I give you my wholehearted permission to raid your own drinks cabinet and join me as I indulge in a little reminiscing.

Did you enjoy as I did the hospital-themed films from the 'Carry On' series, and if so, based on your reading so far, who among the potential liars would you subject to an enema or bed-bath in a bid to get a confession out of them? Again I would maintain dignity in the punishment process – not one to breach ethical nursing standards and all that - although whether or not I could resist the temptation to shove a bunch of daffodils where the sun does not shine is something my conscience is toying with.

Crikey, I have barely taken a swig of my wine as Gobbie is 'ooo, ooo, ooo-ing, he's only doing the conga' back towards the cake judging table, spinning his gravel around like a cheerleader with a pom-pom and high on enthusiasm. I guess that is our cue to get back to basics, but feel free to take your glasses with you.

'Right' starts off Gobbie, 'can the consultant leading the clinical team at the Firchester take her place in the witness box now and tell me her full name and GMC number.'

Having stated her name and number, Vinny reminded Gobbie that first she needed to be sworn in and handed her the Royal Marsden Manual of Clinical Nursing Procedures (Wiley). Having placed on it her hand, which was the size of a baseball glove, consistent with the rest of her frame, she swore to 'tell the truth, the whole truth and whatever' and signed the obligatory attendance register.

Vinny: 'So, lady, you have sworn an oath on a nationally-recognised guide to clinical nursing skills. You claim that you have been a consultant with the Trust for a number of years, so I presume you are familiar with this 'bible', even though it *is* aimed more at nurses than consultants am I right?'

'I guess so,' she said with a seemingly painful squeal and a shrug, her bloodshot eyes resembling the colour of a Bloody Mary. She towered over Vinny's diminutive frame.

Vinny: 'According to the patient's notes you did not actually encounter my client's husband until four days after he was admitted. During that time he was seen by a number of clinicians under your charge. Did you at any point flick back to the start of Ted's admission and query why the initial suspicion of sepsis was crossed off without explanation and replaced with what was little more than a theory based on his medical history without any exploratory tests being carried out?'

Consultant: 'I don't know, can't remember.'

Vinny: 'My client, Ted's widow, wants to know why no investigation was carried out into suspected internal bleeding for which his GP had sent him to you in the first place. What is your explanation for this?'

Consultant: 'I don't know. I wasn't there when he arrived.'

Vinny: 'As the consultant assigned to his care, was it not your job to try to identify why he was admitted in the first place and to carry out the eliminatory checks that the GP was unable to do, and not to presume, nor for your team to assume, what was wrong with him? I have in front of me evidence that shows that none of the markers for advanced liver disease were there, and that your clinicians had little more than an 'impression' of what might have been causing Ted to be so unwell, which was very subjective was it not?'

Consultant: 'I suppose so.'

Vinny: 'You suppose so? Let me ask you then about the blood tests that you ordered on Mr T the night before he died – the only other time you actually encountered your patient, who was little more than a number on a white board. It is my understanding that, as the most senior clinician and specifically the one who ordered the tests, it should have been *your* responsibility to review, act and communicate those results to anyone who was taking over the care of this man. However, it appears that this was not the case. You had not followed up the results, because had you done so then you would have seen how critically unwell Ted had become, and you might have had time to rethink your decision to have him move to any old ward that was free, as it happens, and he might then have got the right treatment to prevent what happened thereafter. What do you say to that?'

Consultant: 'No comment.'

Vinny: At your encounter with Mr T on the fourth day of his admission, you were aware that a CT scan showed that he had, as you put it, 'lung disease and super-added infection.' You would also have been aware that his lactate level was more than double the normal value at that time and that his saturation level was only at 94% breathing room air, which in someone of his age, despite being a smoker, generally hovers around the 98-99% mark. I have asked your team members and now I am asking you: is it not the case that elevated C-reactive protein and lactate levels are two of the clinical values in the scoring system that determine the severity of sepsis in a patient? Is it not also the case that these can lead to a lack of oxygen reaching a person's vital organs, which can cause rapid injury?'

Consultant: 'No comment.'

Vinny: 'Furthermore, is a prolonged capillary refill time of four seconds (peripherally) not a predictor of how the severity of an illness might progress as, and from your own examination of Mr T, it clearly indicates that he fitted this bill? Yet he remained on bog standard antibiotics did he not, which evidently, four days into his admission, had made no difference to his condition, which was in fact worsening. Yet still he was being treated as if his injuries were self-inflicted, based on his lifestyle habit, instead of the necessary treatment having then been initiated. Is that correct? I shall go on,' said Vinny before she could get a word in edgeways.

'Had you carried out your duty as you were supposed to do and looked at those blood results, would you still have considered your patient was in a fit state to be moved from the intensive care unit? Did you pay no attention as to why this man's lactate level had doubled yet again after he arrested, and the fact that he was now unable to breathe on his own? Are you not in the least bit concerned that the very last bit of input you had with Mr T was as one member of the multidisciplinary team, your team of clinicians, who contributed to the decision not to resuscitate this gentleman were he to suffer a subsequent cardiac arrest which he should not have suffered in the first place if only you had checked those results as you should have done? Had you done so, then you would have been in a position to have promptly conveyed to the current team that which needed addressing.'

'My client maintains that neither she nor anyone else in the family was consulted before the resuscitation order was signed. You have stated that she/they *were* aware that Mr T was not going to survive his admission, yet at the time it was signed the family were given every reason to be hopeful, and it was not until over six and a half hours later that they were advised treatment should be stopped. What do you have to say on this matter? Do you still maintain that you had not breached your duty of care over failing to review the blood results that might have led to this man still being alive today? Do you maintain you had adhered to the overriding principles of registration under the General Medical Council to protect your patients from harm?

'Why did Ted's abnormal blood results not stop you from moving him from the safe environment of the Intensive Care Unit to, in essence, a geriatric ward, whereupon he arrested a few hours later? Why afterwards did you tell Ted's wife that elevated lactate levels are normal after someone has arrested, when in fact this was known before the event, yet no one had thought to check the results and follow them up so that this could have properly been acted upon?

'Should Ted's wife, therefore, not have had every right to be concerned by the prejudices and 'presumptive' diagnosis that resulted in her husband being given bog standard antibiotics instead of ones that are specifically designed to target sepsis and to give him the best chance of recovery ,regardless of what was causing him to be septic in the first place, doctors? Does she not equally have a right to be angry at the staff failing to have tried to identify the source of any potential bleeding that would have prompted measures to be taken to minimise any further blood loss and help restore blood circulation to keep him stable?

'Equally, and I will come back to this later on, did you not already know that this man was going to die as soon as it was confirmed, less than half an hour before the DNAR was signed, that the treatment he had been given based on your assumption of the reason for his arrest, which was not in fact true, meant that there was no chance to reverse the effects of medications received? Those medications which would not have been necessary had he not been allowed to arrest in the first place if you had done your job properly?

'Was it not in fact then necessary for your team to quickly put that decision form in place to cover yourselves in the event that this man might arrest again, given what you already knew about the treatment he had undergone – in which you had chosen to conceal many of the facts from the family, not thinking for one minute that your decision would get challenged?'

Consultant: 'It was so long ago, I can't remember now.'

Vinny: 'Well lady, that's a real shame because my client remembers every single detail, and quite frankly I am very irritated by your attempt to maintain your innocence through keeping it tightly buttoned.'

Gobbie was frantically writing this all down, at the same time shaking his head at the consultant and 'tut-tutting', as there was barely a raise of an eyebrow.

'No further questions,' said Vinny, looking daggers at her. It was clear that he wanted her to get the hell out of his sight before he too was on trial for murder.

Vinny's day job is associated with vending machines – automated machines that provide snacks, drinks or the like after money has been inserted. In testing the machines after installation he was used to feeding something into a slot and expecting the right thing to come out. He was struggling therefore to figure out why, when he had so far been feeding the suspects – sorry, persons of interest – such an enormous amount of information, he just could not get a good narrative return for his money.

# EN ROUTE TO VENEZUELA

'Niagara Falls? You're more like Angel Falls with the ferocity of your questioning,' I told Vinny, leaving him to wonder about the comparison. 'Good on you, cuz' I continued. 'You should be proud of yourself. When all this is over I will book us a flight to Venezuela.'

Tentatively I am wondering whether or not we should proceed with questioning the next likely culprit or to put the kettle on, but the latter seems to be a greater need right now. But not so fast, my dears – I need to set you some more 'homework' before you start sipping away on the old PG. I want you to look up sedatives – and I don't mean Nytol or Kalms. I am talking about drugs that have more far-reaching effects and those that must be dispensed and given in a 'controlled' environment. The first one is propofol, the second midazolam, and while you are at it can you also look up morphine, alteplase and atracurium – one being a sedative, one a painkiller, one a blood-thinning agent and the other a muscle relaxant, in that order.

Oh yes, and fragmin (you might find it under the name daltaparin), which is a blood-thinning agent given as an injection. I want you to consider each of these in relation to someone who has suspected internal bleeding, breathing problems and liver disease.

See you in 20 boils of the kettle. Actually, make that 25 – I need to descale the kettle first.

'It's not that I'm afraid to die, I just don't want to be there when it happens' (Woody Allen)

Sorry my love, but you *were* there at the 'scene of the crime.'

'I am dying from the treatment from too many physicians' (Alexander the Great).

Apologies my love, but that is exactly how it was – too many chiefs and not enough Indians.

In handing over to my colleagues on a daily basis, the information that I relay goes way beyond what my clients had for dinner or whether or not they had their bowels opened, as these can easily be checked from both the food and fluid and bowel charts. What is more important is that I effectively communicate information that may not be so readily available without my peers having to read the nursing notes straight off, such as the patient's current condition, any recent changes in their condition (bearing in mind my colleague may have been on leave for a few days), any ongoing treatment they are receiving and what changes they need to look out for that might lead to further complications. Then, and only then, could I be satisfied that I have met my own responsibility to carry out a clear transfer of responsibility.

At the Firchester, no one seemed to take 'ownership' of Ted. With so many different health professionals involved in his care, not only physicians but other members of the multi-disciplinary team, there were gaps in communication, notes were being crossed off and amended left right and centre on his medical file, and there was a general lack of continuity in care, which I believe, greatly contributed to the eventual outcome. The importance of good communication, where it is important, cannot be over-estimated.

Outside of work my family have not been immune to my ability to say stupid things, like the first time I decided to drive to Horsham to visit hubby's family and was over an hour late. When trying to find out where I had gone wrong I told hubby that I had turned left at Govia, and he was baffled. He got out the map and for the life of him could not find any such place, until it transpired that I had actually turned off at a 'go via' junction.

Several years later we actually went to that little

Greek island near Corfu for our fifth wedding anniversary and late honeymoon. Govia did exist, but not on an English motorway.

Then there was the time when hubby and I were courting and we went into a little shop that had home-made jewellery in the window. Whilst pinching my nose I blurted out that the place smelled of 'incest', as joss sticks burned in the windows. He almost died of embarrassment. I knew what I meant of course. He then sought to test my knowledge further by asking me if I knew incest was a game all the family could play.

And yes, I have interpreted things wrongly in the past, such as the time when hubby was discussing with a farmer the best kind of lawnmower to buy at a local fair, as I listened on attentively. As the farmer proceeded to explain to Ted that 'this one is a 12-inch cut' or 'this one is an 18-inch cut' and he had decided the latter was the one for us, I innocently piped up, 'We don't need that one because I don't let the grass grow that high'. (I was the one who had cut the lawn from the moment we got married and who was stuck with job thereafter). Well, the look on both their faces was priceless, and me – well I did not know what I had said wrong until we got home and was told in no uncertain terms by Ted to leave the talking to him in future.

And as for the time when I took the kids to the opening of a new shopping centre in Bridgwater, where we lived in 1986, well!

'What did you do today, my love?' Ted asked when he got home from work.

'Not much' I said, 'just the usual things and then we went to Angel Place, where we saw the Queen.'

'Did you get a good look at her?' Ted asked.

'Yes I did' I replied. 'She looked great. She cut the ribbon and then left soon after, followed by her dysenteries.' I meant 'dignitaries' of course, I knew that, but my series of faux pas became the talk of the town from then onwards. Hubby could never resist telling all his workmates of the latest seemingly ignoramus thing I had come out with, but he would also say that was what he loved about me – my stupid innocence.

But the point in these scenarios is that I did not get lost in the end and there were no immoral undertakings in that shop. It took me half the time to cut the lawn, thanks to those few extra inches, and thank god Her Majesty's entourage did not have the runs after all.

I am not as stupid as I sound. I know the difference in the purity of gold and I know that the impurity of hubby's death investigation has been nothing short of a 24-carat cock-up.

# THE HANDOVER

—◦⬥◦—

'Can you get Vinny to put the nurse through her paces next?' I ask Gobbie, who confers with my cousin to ensure my wishes are carried out. With that it is time for me to step aside once more and let my 'chappy' get on with what he does best – interrogating. I have no idea what this nurse looks like or even if it is a she, although the name on the paperwork suggests it is, as my mind conjures up the closing scene from the Waltons:

'Night Mary Ellen, night ma, night John Boy' says Vinny, barely able to contain his delight at his own wicked sense of humour, which tends to run in the family. Having then composed himself he puts on a very serious voice and calls for the nurse who was had been responsible for taking over the care of Ted on the night in question.

Before you get any more warped Fifty Shades images in your mind, Gobbie had blind-folded me before leading me towards a chair outside the tent where I now sit, for no other reason than that he knew that once I set eyes on the nurse I would not be able to stop myself pushing a hot poker into her pupils. After all, it was she who was blind to hubby's abnormal ECG reading, and Gobbo was worried I might find an' ironically' good way to pay her back. However, two wrongs don't make a right, and I *am* keen to keep my own PIN number intact.

As a student nurse I was taught that one's hearing is the last of the senses to go. Just because I was blindfolded it did not mean that I would not be able to hear what was being said, so when I heard her voice, and it was a 'her', I could not help thinking I had heard it before. Having been asked to swear on a copy of *Night at the Museum* (the Firchester being a very old building and all that), in her version of 'telling the truth, the whole truth and whatever', she sounded remarkably like Mammy (aka Hattie McDaniel from *Gone with the Wind*), but then it couldn't possibly have been her because she died in 1952. Otherwise it would have been more appropriate for her to swear on Margaret Mitchell's epic novel.

Perhaps it was the fact the Vinny had just got back from the plantation that my mind was all over the place. Finally things were getting under way.

Vinny: 'You were the night nurse on duty at the Firchester on the night in question, were you not?'

Nurse: 'Yes I's-a-was,' she said with a southern twang.

Vinny: In what state was Mr T when he arrived on your ward just after 10pm?'

Nurse: 'I have no idea.'

Vinny: 'You have no idea? Pardon me if I am speaking out of turn, but I assumed that since you are built like an elephant your memory would follow suit.' Am I to understand then that instead, you have the retentive memory of a gnat?'

Listening from the sidelines I envisaged someone with extremely wrinkled skin and a large hooter. Gobbie went into Cheshire cat mode again, but was aware he needed to bring order to the court.

Gobbie (to Vinny): 'That was out of order. Give the poor woman something to wipe her tears with' he said, as liquid golf balls trickled down her fat cheeks. With that Vinny handed her a tablecloth, hoping it would be big enough.

Vinny: 'Since you have come here with no clue as to why, let me take you back to that night. The gentleman in question was transferred on a large amount of oxygen and it was your job to monitor his condition, and you reported that he was 'awake and alert' at the time. Your report further states that this gentleman complained of feeling unwell after he had used the communal bathroom, for which you documented a significant amount of blood loss; that he had become breathless on return to bed thereafter and complained of chest pain.

'In your write up you say that you carried out an electrocardiogram, which is a way of recording someone's heart rhythm and detecting any abnormalities. However, the chest pain, it seems, happened before he went to the bathroom, as the ECG print-outs show the exact time it was done. Yet, despite the fact that it showed an abnormal reading that sent out signals of an emergency, you failed to contact a doctor or other medical professional on your ward with immediate effect. Had you done so then treatment could have been started based on their own interpretation.

'I suggest you did not feel it necessary to report this, as you knew the doctor would be doing his normal ward round at some point and you paid no heed either to the information that had been documented on the Early Warning Score, which, with a score of 5 or above, indicates a severe medical emergency, as was also the case.

Was it not some fifty minutes later before you actually encountered that doctor and told him only of the chest pain mentioned by the patient, upon which he then prescribed among other things a high dose of aspirin? You failed to inform him about his trip to the bathroom didn't you, regardless of the new prescription?'

I was proud of Vinny. Not once had he paused for breath.

Nurse: 'I don't know.'

'Then I shall refresh your memory,' continued Vinny, checking the medication chart in front of him.

'Upon medication being prescribed, you did then take those drugs to Mr T and he took them, but literally within seconds of doing so you found him to be unresponsive. You had already confirmed the medications had been taken by your signature on the medication chart, yet you claimed that he had not actually taken the aspirin since he was 'not awake'. Yet he was awake at the very same time he took those other medicines for which you had also signed as having been taken. How do you explain that, and your alteration to the drug chart? Is this not a legal document? Am I right in thinking that charts, and medication charts in particular, act as a description of the facts at the time and could act as a 'persuasive witness' in a court of law?

'Are you aware that you could have your licence revoked if you are found guilty of altering medical records, falsifying records or making incorrect entries from a legal perspective? Shall I go on?' says Vinny, looking to Gobbie for confirmation, which he gets.

Vinny: 'So here was this patient, on your shift, who had an ECG reading which indicated that a heart attack was likely, who evidently was bleeding internally and who you had given a high dose blood thinning drug to (the aspirin) just before you found him 'unresponsive', yet you seek to take no responsibility for having failed to summon help for which a doctor might have prescribed what is called a beta-blocker (a tablet that could have got this man's heart back to a normal rhythm) in the first instance, yet you chose not to, which then led to this unfortunate event.

'You gave also to Mr T, did you not, glyceryl tinitrate after the doctor had prescribed it – a treatment used where someone is suspected of having angina, yet Ted had complained only of chest pain, which could quite easily have been indigestion or muscle strain, could it not? Given as a couple of sprays at first under the tongue, it should not, however, be given where a person has low blood pressure or problems with their liver or kidneys. Ted's low blood pressure was the primary concern all the way along, with low urinary output and an already scarred liver, yet this did not deter you from giving him this, did it, despite the reading on the Early Warning Chart. Is this something else I should be expected to ignore?

'Do you not consider, given all this, that you were wholly responsible for this man having arrested, an arrest from which he never recovered? Do you not consider you were clinically negligent and should be punished for not one, not two, not even three but four counts of incompetence?

Nurse: 'You have got it all wrong. I am sure that is not how it was.'

Vinny: Does the Nursing and Midwifery Council Code in relation to keeping clear and accurate records not apply to you?'

Nurse: 'Of course, why do you ask?'

Vinny: The 'how' comes at section 10(1), where it says 'all records must be completed as soon as possible after an event'an event'. The times you have recorded about when medication was prescribed do not tally with the medical notes and if, in conformation with Section (10)1 of the Nursing and Midwifery code, you had recorded the administration of medication at the time it was actually taken, not given, why did you then seek to back-track after it had become evident that all had not been well with your patient?

More seriously at 10(3), does it not say 'all records should be completed accurately and without any falsification'? I suggest you realised you had made a mistake by giving Mr T the aspirin, aware that it would have caused additional bleeding and therefore, fearful that the mistake would be uncovered at a later date. This prompted you to alter the medicine chart in the same way.

Vinny could not help but focus at that particular moment on her big hooked nose, thinking any minute now she was going to open her mouth and it was going to straighten up and extend to the point where she might struggle to get it through the opening of the tent.

'I am sure I didn't get things wrong' she said.

'You know this runs a lot deeper,' said Vinny, 'but not all these matters can be addressed here today. You are free to leave the court, but don't leave the country,' he told her as she slithered away.

# TRUTH INJECTION

———⟨✕⟩———

So Ted arrested, and without getting too technical, the emergency team carried out CPR on him. After a rather significant amount of time they had apparently 'restored spontaneous circulation' – in other words 'brought him back from the dead.' Yet this was not necessarily the case.

Because he had complained of chest pain, and not having all the other information that the night nurse had failed to hand over, including the fact that the aspirin *had* in fact been given, he was then given medication to treat what they thought was a blood clot on his lungs – a 'pulmonary embolism', they called it. Not any old medication, I might add, but more blood thinning agents, and let us not forget why he had gone to the Firchester in the first place.

Vinny: 'Your Judgeship' he said, 'I shall now call the anaesthetist to the gazebo.'

Whilst the record shows that two different anaesthetists tended to Ted after his arrest, only one had been selected by the Trust to represent this particular discipline.

'Wow' says Gobbie, his ears pricking up. 'I met her before on the dance floor when my brother was in *that* show.' He was interested to know how she fitted into the 'trial.' Having quickly gone on his laptop in search of any newspaper article that might link her to this case, he inadvertently clicked on a You Tube channel instead, and the tent shook at the volume with which he had it set: 'I'm outta love, set me free, and let me out this misery, show me the way to get...'

At which point Vinny intervened.

Vinny: 'Gobbie my man, what are you doing?'

'What do you mean?' replied the fake barrister, licking his digit finger and brushing it over his eyebrows.

Vinny: 'I said I was going to call the anaesthetist, not Anastacia!' At that point Vinny wondered exactly what might have been in his tea, because he was certainly on a roll when it came to making jokes.

'Sorry Vinny boy' Gobbie said, sniggering, claiming that he was a trifle deaf on account of having jelly and cream in one of his ears and sponge and custard in the other. Hey, I was thinking to myself, I used that joke back in the seventies!

Thank god it wasn't Anastacia on the stand, I was thinking, else I know she would have razzle-dazzled Robbie's bro' into letting her off, and besides, if she thought she could waltz herself into his good books she would have to think again, because if anyone was going after that glitterball trophy with the diamante scales of justice on top, it was going to be me.

Booboo over, or should I say 'misunderstanding' (since I am into comparatives right now), Vinny summoned the anaesthetist, Dr. Numbty, to pledge an oath on a copy of the *Washington Post*, specifically the article in which the controversy over Michael Jackson's death was slapped on the front pages.

Anaesthetist: 'I swear to tell the truth, the whole truth and whatever' said she, having first signed the attendance record.

Vinny was trying to link his own conspiracy theory to the fact that this, the fifth suspect in the case of Hubby T, had used the exact same words when being sworn in as her colleagues before her. Now that's what you call collaborative working.

Vinny: 'The records show that within twenty minutes of Mr T having been resuscitated following a respiratory (not cardiac as it happens) arrest, you did insert a laryngoscopy into his windpipe so as to facilitate tracheal intubation, as he was not able to maintain his own airway properly, is that correct? Is it not also a very uncomfortable procedure?'

Anaesthetist: 'I can't remember.'

'Well you did,' said Vinny. 'The records then show that at that point he received no anaesthetic agents and that soon afterwards an arterial line was inserted into his radial artery which presumably was so that his blood pressure could be monitored and for ease of arterial blood gas sampling.'

Ted's widow was somewhat confused, as she could not see the necessity for her husband to have received morphine or midazolam at that point, as the line was, according to the notes, sited without complications at first attempt. Yet she was told by the consultant leading the team that they were given because he had become agitated, and were given as 'comfort measures' for his journey back to the Intensive Care Unit, which he should never have left in the first place.

'What is your recollection of this?' asked Vinny.

'I can't remember,' replied the anaesthetist, which took Vinny by surprise, as he was convinced that the qualities an anaesthetist needed to possess included an ability to think quickly and methodically under pressure.

Vinny: 'Then let me remind you doctor, and perhaps at the same time you could clear a few things up for us. Is midazolam not meant to be a short-acting anxiety-reducing drug with the emphasis being on 'short-acting? Is it not also a drug that works within minutes? Is it not also a drug that needs to be given in as small a quantity as necessary and gradually increased at intervals only when necessary, and someone should not be given the maximum safe dose of 5mgs in one go, as Mr T's record shows was done?'

The woman standing in front of him, who looked like a cross between Betty Boop with her button nose and careful coiffure and Jessica Rabbit with her flaming Veronica Lake hairstyle and wasp waist, might not conform to the usual stereotypical look of a numbing 'agent', yet it was obvious by her demeanour that she was hostile towards anyone accusing her of wrong-doing. She did not come over as naïve enough to think that an inadvertent error in the delivery of medical care might be recognised as anything other than an important feature when it came to patient morbidity or mortality, and this was becoming evident to Vinny, who could see her reluctance to drop herself or her colleagues in it.

Fortunately for me, whilst Vinny did love the ladies, his first loyalty was to me, so he was not about to let this gorgeous specimen flirt with him, and besides he wasn't particularly struck on her steely grey eyes, which looked a little shifty.

'Exactly how much midazolam did you give this man, doctor? The medication chart suggests it could have been double that amount, yet it is not clear, because you have made a very heavy amendment in an attempt to cover up what is written underneath. Is it not illegal, doctor, to falsify medication charts?'

Dr Numbty remained composed but said nothing.

Vinny: Ignore the issue if you will doctor, but does the BNF not state that midazolam can cause severe respiratory depression, that it should be used 'cautiously' in anyone who has a history of alcohol use and that it can cause a severe drop in blood pressure in anyone who has, or is even suspected of having, internal bleeding (hypovolaemia)?

'In the first instance, am I to believe that you were totally unaware that Mr T had, prior to his arrest, taken 300mgs aspirin and received daltaparin, both which are designed to thin the blood, only then to be given alteplase after his arrest, which would have thinned his blood further, not considering for one minute that this was a lethal combination, given the other issue as I have already mentioned? Is it any wonder his blood pressure would not pick up?

'Lastly doctor Numpty, I mean Numbty – does morphine not also cause respiratory depression and a decrease in blood pressure which would have further compounded the situation? Did you not then give my client's husband a 'double whammy' of inappropriate sedation? Should doses of anaesthetic not also take into account a person's body weight at the time, and Mr T was not a particularly big man?'

There was nothing the anaesthetist could say at that point, and to pardon the expression she seemed quite insensitive to anything that had been fired her way.

Vinny: 'Your Judgeship, do I have your permission to continue this line of inquiry? In the words of Jimmy Cricket, 'there's more.'

Gobbie: 'Proceed.'

Vinny: 'So we have established, doc, that Mr T was sedated by you following insertion of the arterial line. Only it did not end there, did it? An hour later you, or perhaps it was your colleague, who chose not be here today, made three attempts at putting a line into his internal jugular vein. This is a very dangerous procedure, is it not, with the potential for arterial puncture if not inserted correctly, is that right? I suggest that this is exactly what happened to Mr T, albeit you likely did not intend to mess things up. You see, it's just that the pathology reports confirm it had become displaced, among other things.

'Likely you were not on the ward when this man's family complained about bleeding from the neck only hours before he died. None of the staff seemed fazed by it, but did happen.

'Going back to your role doctor, the record shows that while this man was sedated on morphine and midazolam, either you or one of your assisting colleagues did, at the point of finishing the internal jugular vein insertion, administer to Mr T propofol intravenously – not once but twice, as was signed for by you both. This is the normal process where controlled drugs are concerned, is it not? Is it not the case also that propofol is a sedative-hypnotic drug that causes sleep within seconds yet can also cause respiratory depression or total airway compromise, in the same way as midazolam?'

'Yes, but...' replied the redhead, but her sentence was cut short by Vinny.

'But, but, but,' mimicked Vinny, 'is it normally the case, doctor, that where propofol is administered without other anaesthetic drugs the patient should normally wake up within minutes of it being discontinued? But there again, Mr T continued to receive every hour on the hour propofol and morphine intravenously between then and within up to half an hour of his machine then being turned off – the decision that was made by one of your associates, herself an anaesthetist – so it seems to me more likely than not that this chap was already brain dead by that time.

'The Consultant was your friend, was she not? We have heard her account today, yet she was not able to offer any explanation as to why her patient should have died, or is that what she decided to write on her notes, to protect you and your fellow anaesthetist? This man, doctor, further received a medication called atracurium which is mostly advantageous, is it not, where a person's muscles start to twitch, and therefore as a muscle relaxant this would seek to prevent this from happening? Could it have been then that the endotracheal intubation process was so distressing for Mr T that he was given this drug on top of everything else to help calm him down? But is it not also the case that this drug can cause severe hypotension (decrease in blood pressure) as one of the main side effects?

'I am sure you are fully aware, doctor, the steps my client has gone to in order to find out exactly what dose was given and at what time, yet how is it that all access has been denied? What do you and your colleagues have to hide? Could it be that this too contributed to an overdose of medication? And why is it that it took my client's widow years before the Trust admitted to her husband having been given midazolam at all, having denied it on more than one occasion, yet it has at no point committed in writing to exactly how much he was given, given the drug chart has been overwritten so that the original entry is illegible? And what of oxygen toxicity – over-oxygenation? Mr T was transferred to the ward from ICU on 10 litres of oxygen, was he not? That is an awful lot of oxygen, and my research suggests that an accidental overdose of a number of different kinds of medication can cause a pulseless arrest.'

Just so as you know readers, pulseless electrical activity (PEA) is a clinical condition characterized by unresponsiveness and no palpable pulse, but with some organised cardiac electrical activity. It is different from what you might know as a cardiac arrest in the true sense.

'Your colleague, the consultant, has openly confessed that this chap's blood pressure was not improving, nor was it likely to after the critical hours had passed. Given the circumstances, you have to ask yourself why not, don't you doc?'

Anaesthetist: 'No comment.'

Vinny: 'You have openly sworn on the article about Michael Jackson to tell the truth, the whole truth and whatever. Given the same scenario, do Mr T's medical notes also suggest that the 'milk of amnesia' that had been given involuntarily, unlike that of MJ's choosing, went a little further than just propofol?'

Whilst Ted was not averse to the odd glass of Baileys over ice, unlike the egg-white colour of propofol, he had it on very few occasions. Yet even if he had drunk a whole litre neat, it would not have rendered him unconscious. I too have enjoyed sampling the cream-coloured delight, but there really can be no comparison.

There was always the potential for MJ to overdose on propofol – the Bailey's equivalent – and especially when mixed with alcohol, as had happened in his case.

The anaesthetist(s) looking after Ted had a duty of care to ensure the effects of an over- abundance of medication were controlled, yet they went right ahead and gave him a triple cocktail that was far from suitable. However, Ted's story will not make front page news.

Why not? Because in English Law 'manslaughter by gross negligence' needs to cover four elements, which in relation to an anaesthetist alone would be: (a) did the person owe a duty of care to Hubby T? (b) had the person breached that duty of care? (c) if the person had, then did this cause the death of Hubby T? And (d), was the breach so 'gross that it showed such disregard for life and the safety of others as to amount to a crime and deserving of punishment?'

As Brooke, I have come to my own conclusion on matters, given the circumstances so far, and these would be, in alphabetical order, yes they did, yes they did, it heavily contributed, and that whilst I am not vindictive enough to think that there was intention by anyone to disregard Ted's life, what is a 'crime' worthy of punishment in some form or another is how collectively those who looked after him had extended the lies, or had been reticent with the truth, with other people and organisations that fell outside of the workings of the Firchester when I went looking for additional support.

Hold these thoughts for later on, but please to not take it that I am trying to influence your decision one way or the other.

Having seemingly become numb to all the questioning, Vinny felt it pointless keeping the anaesthetist standing in the miniature gazebo any longer and suggested she go and get a face transplant – one that would portray someone who gave a damn.

Gobbie reads out to all of you involved in the decision making process: 'A form of strict, secondary liability that arises under the common law doctrine of agency, *respondeat superior* (let the master answer), the responsibility of the superior for the acts of their subordinate or, in a broader sense, the responsibility of any third party that had the 'right, ability or duty to control' the activities of a violator'. This is the Wiki definition of 'vicarious liability', but feel free to research others. To put it simply, this means that whoever is ultimately responsible for the actions or inactions of the staff under their employ must be the ones to stand trial, and this was Vinny's cue to get the chief executive officer up next. Ironically she was, as usual nowhere to be found, at first.

'Hickory, dickory 'doc'. Where is the chief mouse that ran up the clock (the clock face being the litigation authority)? The place where the clock struck one hell of a deal with her (drain the wife's batteries until they run out).

That mouse ran down (confident she would win). And that's why she will never face that hickory, dickory dock. A bit corny I know, but then 'scepticism is as scepticism does,' I am thinking to myself angrily.

But wait, what is that noise? As Gobbie and Vinny leave their tables for a split second and rush outside, lo and behold, sitting behind the wheel of a red 1956 Maserati 450S prototype, is a woman with a leopard-print headscarf and oversized sunglasses, and it wasn't for the fact that her earrings are diamond studded instead of pearls she could so easily be mistaken for Audrey Hepburn. That is, until she opens her mouth, which is definitely minus a plum.

'What's up, pet?' says the woman, having turned the engine off and painstakingly wound the window down. She is making direct eye contact with my cousin.

'That depends on who you are,' replies Vinny, getting all hot under the collar. She confirms she is the head honcho who is due to take the stand next.

Vinny was a sucker for a Geordie accent and he could tell right away that she was a woman who knew how to use her charms to facilitate her own end. She was not what he had expected. When he had read the pre-trial notes about her being the 'queen bee' at the Firchester he visualised someone short and blonde with a distinctive cockney accent, but now he realised where he had gone wrong. His thoughts had deviated towards the queen of the Vic, so in some ways he was relieved; at least he (and the rest of you) would not have to be exposed to her bikini top flying off during extensive exercising of her jaw during questioning at the risk of my book having to be given an adult rating (*Carry on Camping*, 1969).

Vinny was fully aware that this was the woman

who had stolen my chance of any kind of resolution and had wished for a moment that he was the investigating detective and not me. He relished the thought of being able to frisk her down to see where she was hiding all the lies, and knowing my cousin to be a 'leg man', he would most definitely have started with her ankles and worked his way upwards, taking particular care not to have missed anything.

But I had already sized her up, and she had already been briefed by her legal team, especially as I insisted she must speak for herself and not rely on any representation.

Composed and ready to take on this beguiling beauty, Vinny got the ball rolling.

Vinny: 'Place your hand on a copy of your job contract and quote after me,' he said, hoping that he would not go into a hypnotic trance after one waft of her expensive and overpowering perfume.

'I swear to tell the truth, the whole truth and whatever' she said, and signed the attendance record that was thrust upon her.

'Where did you get the Maserati from?' Vinny asked. 'And how much did it cost you, if you don't mind me asking?' He was forgetting for one minute where he was.

'In Monte Carlo,' she replied, 'and let's just say that I paid a fair few francs for it back in the day.' She was giving little away except to confirm that the fiery red number had run into six figures.

'It is fair to say then that you have always been on a pretty good salary then?' Vinny asked inquisitively, wondering exactly what she did to earn it. 'Anyway,' he continued, 'Ted's wife submitted to you, as head of the establishment, a formal complaint letter in which she gave an extensive account of the care and treatment that her husband received whilst under the care of the medical team for which you are ultimately accountable ,did she not?'

Chief Executive: 'So I believe.'

Vinny: 'So this letter was sent to you less than four months after the gentleman died, and despite her being in the early stages of grieving she poured her heart out to you about the contradictions in treatment, medication, diagnosis and what had come out of the post mortem. Are you telling me you do not remember reading that letter?'

'If you say so,' she replied.

'Well, I do,' Vinny said. He then remarked on the letter she had written to Mr T shortly afterwards to say how sorry she was to hear of those concerns and how she had asked that the widow accept her condolences at that 'sad time'.

Chief Executive: 'I do not deal with complaints myself but pass any concerns onto my clinical team to deal with.'

Well, yes, as Mum used to say, what is the point of getting a dog and then barking yourself?

Vinny: 'Your people [the administrative department], wrote to Mr T's widow on your behalf to say that someone would investigate what happened, yet all that happened was that you selected only a minor concern among the most serious of accusations in which a brief yet unacceptable explanation was given. I suggest it was for no other reason than that you had been sent a copy of a letter which Mrs T had sent to the Coroner's officer in confidence with explicit details about the care and treatment this man received whilst in your charge, and therefore you had been forewarned of the implications, which would put the Trust in a very awkward situation. Now does it jog any memories?'

Chief Executive: 'Not specifically.'

Vinny: 'Then I suggest you have a very short memory, madam, because it was less than a year ago when you last wrote to Mrs T. You continued to turn a blind eye and close matters at your end suggesting she seek advice from a solicitor if she was 'not happy', yet knowing full well that there would be no point to this given the time that has elapsed, which you were already fully aware of. There *was* no investigation, was there? And if there was, then I suggest it was little more than general chit-chat among your team, none of which was actually recorded, in written or any other form, as Mrs T has managed to find out at source.

'You did not report this as a serious untoward incident, did you? Because you knew that if you did and if it were the case that this man actually had sepsis when he arrived at your hospital, then there would be no end of questions being raised as to how this was mismanaged. You were not concerned about any further risk to other patients, only the risk of litigation as a result of someone having died under your charge, which, in line with hospital policy, had the highest of ratings, a 'red' rating, did it not?

'I suggest you showed total disregard for both the patient and his family throughout an investigation initiated by an outside body by attempting to cover up any wrong-doing, starting with allowing it to go unchallenged as to why this man's initial diagnosis of sepsis was crossed off in favour of a condition that you were determined to link to his medical history as your 'get out' clause. The most important issue of all, the internal bleeding, was not investigated nor treated appropriately.'

She showed no remorse, rolling her eyes and checking her nail polish for cracks.

It is at this point that I handed Gobbie a note to tell him Vinny was wasting his breath today. She was evidently not going to say anything that might incriminate herself or the Firchester.

Vinny reminded her that she was the one responsible for 'signing off' the complaint response letters to Mrs T, so she should be the one to take responsibility for doing little more than skirting around the most serious of issues within a very complex case in the hope that Mr T's widow would succumb to this and go away.

Yet again my mind was wandering back to my childhood. Unable to afford carpet for the hallway in that little council flat in north London, dad would instead get down on his hands and knees and apply red cardinal polish to the tiles, which left them looking nice and shiny. It needed to be applied evenly, else it would look messy, and I soon perfected the art when helping to touch it up now and again. All we really sought to do was to cover over the cracks to hide any imperfections left by the council. Similarly, the Firchester could not afford to risk the reputational or financial damage that a clinical negligence case might bring. As I continued to expose the flaws in the workings of the hospital outside of that setting, it was evident that things were starting to get a bit messy. Utilising their legal privileges, the management and her team had perfected the art of painting for themselves a picture of perfection over any flaws in Ted's health, and after a series of cardinally polished manoeuvres on their part, I was the one who was beginning to crack up.

But Vinny wasn't finished with her quite yet. He had one more ace up his sleeve and he was going to use it to his advantage. With Mr T's medical notes to hand and having done his homework, he was keen to question this Trust's ultimate leader about the death of a person under anaesthetic. He had looked into the policy rule that governs this, which state: 'whenever someone dies within 48 hrs following the administration of an anaesthetic agent, or as the result of any complications arising from the administration of such an anaesthetic, the fact of death needs reporting without delay to the Executive Director for Public Health by the person who actually administered that anaesthetic to the deceased.'

He wanted to find out why this was not done, given Ted had died around 16 hours after having received the drugs as described earlier, and he also wanted to find out who it was who decided which witnesses should have attended the inquest – her or the Coroner – and why this particular aspect of Ted's treatment had not been documented or investigated, leave aside everything else.

'I have read Mr T's medical records,' Vinny told her, 'and especially your letters. It seems to me that you love to quote procedures, yet it would appear to me, madam, that despite this you are happy to sit in your office polishing your brass inkwell despite accusations against your staff, fully confident that no matter how much a complainant hits you with, you can rest assured your house will not burn down.

'I have to say that when you turned up in your car looking the way you did that you appeared a woman of substance, but your lack of empathy and reluctance to own up to anything remotely untoward proves to me that you cannot judge a book by its cover. You seriously need to re-educate yourself on morals and values.'

It is unfortunate for me that Alfred Hitchcock isn't among my virtual 'jury' right now to give you a few solving tips– after all this is turning out to be a right *Charade*, isn't it? Instead I shall have to keep you in 'suspenders', I mean suspense, for a wee bit longer, but hey, if the cap fits…

# GEPPETTO'S BOYS

———◦◦◦———

Talking of caps fitting, falsifying evidence to procure the conviction of someone honestly believed to be guilty is considered a form of corruption in the policing world, yet allegations of individual clinical negligence can so easily be dressed up as systematic failures where no one is made to face the consequences. Does this seem fair?

So now you all know what happened to Ted after he went for a routine visit to the quacks and Vinny had reeled the 'persons of interest' in hook, line and sinker. I do not live in the Black Hills, The Black Hills of Dakota, but it has been necessary for me to share with you all the dark side of professional ethics in order to pull something meaningful out of such a tragedy. A calamity in fact that should never have happened as they whip-cracked away, whip-cracked away, whip-cracked away at closing the curtains on what had become a 'Dead (wood)' stage. (Doris Day, *Calamity Jane* 1953).

As his personal representative (the unromantic title that has been bestowed upon me in replacement for 'the wife') I consider I have every right to make this legal declaration of what I perceive to have happened to Ted in whatever form it takes, as the weight of all this has been hanging around my neck like one of the lead aprons that I have frequently worn as a radiation shield when taking a patient for an X-ray. I had managed to pull all this out of my top hat whether it were at the 55¾ stage, the 56¾ stage or until now, yet for all the notice anyone has taken of me you would think I had presented them with a blank piece of parchment. Is it any wonder I have been going potty?

As that lonely widow detective then, how do you think I have done? As Brooke, have I done a good job of keeping my tears from bubbling to the surface while scurrying around the courtroom like a sheepdog?

George Bernard Shaw (1856-1950) once said 'life does not cease to be funny when people die, any more than it ceases to be serious when people laugh', and for a split second I am wondering how Piggy Malone and Charlie Farley would have handled this case (*The Two Ronnies)* – likely there would have been a lot of raspberry blowing.

But Ted's death was no laughing matter, any more

than the joke about the short-sighted man who walked into a hospital with two burned ears and had to explain to the doctor that whilst ironing his shirt he had stopped to let his dog in from the garden and put the iron down on the telephone table, only to pick the iron up instead of the phone when he heard it ring. Then he did it again, putting the iron to his other ear. So it is a funny story, but neglecting to treat the burns to his ears in a timely manner could lead to cosmetic deformity of varying degrees, let alone affect the quality of his life. The chap won't die, but the nerves in his ears might. How would the clinicians get out of that, one has to wonder?

The simple truth is that if you tell someone there is wet paint on a wall, invariably they will touch it just to see. Try to tell someone about clinical negligence and they will avoid the issue altogether in case there is a chemical reaction! In essence, what happened in my case was that the Trust chose to 'gloss' over it (pun intended) and was careful not to leave thumb prints.

Do you think me an awful cow for pouring my heart out to the world like this, or does any of this kind of behaviour strike a chord with you?

So this is the worse bit over. Vinny has laid my case before you and now it is up to you to decide the who, what, when and where, although it really isn't rocket science, is it? Apologies to all you rocket scientists out there by the way – please don't launch me into oblivion.

Now I need to round this story up properly, so please keep your specs on for a while longer. Imagine a kaleidoscope – if you haven't seen one, it's a tube with a selection of mirrors where lots of loose colourful objects float around at the bottom and get all mixed up when the dial at the top is turned or it is shaken up; basic, but great fun as a kid. In the kaleidoscope of care, the picture was not quite so pretty. There has been no light at the end of that tunnel, only a reflection of the emotional and heartbroken woman that is me as those responsible for hubby's death had somehow got their stories mixed up over mine.

Going back to the cottage or shepherd's pie scenario, in Medieval and Renaissance cookery, whether it was beef or lamb that was used, before the mash was dolloped on top the minced meat would also have been sitting on a layer of mash enclosed within a pastry crust. It was all about trial and error I guess as to whether or not the pastry case actually made any difference, yet it would seem not, since the modern-day cookbooks have done away with it.

This pastry crust was referred to as a 'coffyn', by the way – ironic don't you think, as for that poor Hindu patient choking on the guilt of having eaten beef instead of mince earlier on in my tale it could quite easily have been the death of his cultural reputation. That reminds me of a saying that one of my patients regularly comes out with: 'It wasn't the cough that carried him off but the coffin they carried him off in.'

Likewise, one would have thought that nursing would have progressed a long way since the Middle Ages, but during the course of my journey to find the truth I have not found this to be the case. Having openly admitted that they did not know exactly what hubby's illness was, he was at a disadvantage, and his life was lost through a series of missed diagnoses, misdiagnoses and medication errors.

Concentrations of drugs in blood can be so useful for establishing recent drug ingestion whether in tablet form or given intravenously (especially anaesthetics). From them a pathologist would be able to determine the effect of a drug on a deceased person at the post mortem. A toxicology report would have prevented him from second-guessing, yet wrongly portrayed by the clinicians in Ted's medical notes as an alcohol abuser and chain smoker, that is exactly what the pathologist did when he had so little else to go on.

Timelines are considered to be the preferred visual aid for lawyers and legal beagles who have a need to chronologically demonstrate the facts and events of a case – a way of supporting their verbal arguments. Ordinarily there is nothing to be gained from a coroner calling witnesses to court to give oral evidence, as generally he would conclude an inquest based on documentary evidence, yet contrary to Rule 23 under the Coroners (Inquest) Rules 2013 they were called to give their version of events, the version I had so passionately contested over the preceding year or more. It was not so much a 'trial' as an informal 'hearing' from which the Coroner then delivered his conclusion in a narrative form, having been sucked in by their lies.

So the death certificate gave the cause of death as

being multi-organ failure in the end, after I had gone full circle.

In wrapping up my case then, I need you to consider whether multi-organ dysfunction syndrome or multi-organ failure is the right terminology to use. The difference is that with multi-organ dysfunction syndrome two organs can fail at the same time, but I wonder exactly what those two might have been in Ted's case, since that very same verdict confirmed 'no evidence of liver failure'. Ironic, don't you think?

Trying to get to the bottom of hubby's death is driving me to an early grave – but at least I have my Wizard of Oz inspired coffyn – I mean coffin – to fall back on (or should I say, into)!

Maybe I ought to have known long ago when to shut up and stop looking for answers as I continued to battle with the locals, extended would-be helpers, and even a very uncompromising judge in the highest of chambers, but I just cannot give up trying to unravel the mystery of who was responsible for taking my hubby away from me. I cannot settle for him telling me that there is 'nothing to be gained' from a second inquest despite four extra years of evidence that could put this baby to rest once and for all, so pardon me if I do not take any notice of the man behind the curtain (*Wizard of Oz*, 1939.) As my last port of call I naively relived on him being able to us his magical powers to conjure up a proper investigation, but instead he sent me packing back down that yellow brick road.

Before I even reached that point I encountered along the way those who are paid to regulate activities within health and social care; to represent their local constituents within a political party; to create national policies and legislations in relation to health and social care; to uphold information rights; and those who claim they can make final decisions on complaints that have not been resolved by the NHS, government or other public bodies free of cost, all to no avail.

I was always under the notion that Pinocchio was an only child, yet in the course of complaining, and in the abbreviated world of political organisations, I came across a whole heap of others just like him with the very same affliction – Geppetto's boys, I like to call them. Their promises to 'help people have their voices heard in government and parliament', to 'listen to people to understand their needs and tailor services accordingly', to 'provide an independent high-quality complaint handling service that rights individual wrongs' and to 'make sure that health and social care services provide people with safe, effective, competent and high quality care' never materialised. Approach any one of them with concerns over clinical negligence within the system, as I did, and miraculously this type of complaint does not 'fall within their remit at individual level' - that they 'cannot deal with individual complaints.'

How then are things supposed to be put right when they are not interested in learning how the wrongs occurred in the first place? Is it not as simple as that? All I have tried to do is to be a good advocate for seeking a change in the way the law works when it comes to equality in care. Just call me 'Flo' – the fur-lined caped crusader!

On my previous fictitious journey to the Emerald City I remember the good witch Glinda telling me that I 'always had the power (dear) but that I just never knew it.' Did she mean the power to get to the bottom of an investigation, to become a good writer and recruit a whole heap of strangers into her fairy tale, or to become a saint, I wonder?

Nevertheless, the power is now in my hands in one way, as I can use my writing as a legitimate platform to vent my anger and frustration in a hopefully not too depressive way. And no, before you ask, I do not wear my bloomers on the outside of my 10 denier tights, because one huge gust of wind and I might find myself in orbit.

When I said I hated board games it was not strictly true, as there *is* one that I have kept in reserve that I can share in my summing up.

In my 'vintage' years I came across a classic newspaper and reporter's game by Waddington that was buried in a box in the garage somewhere between my equally old collection of trolls and a pile of Dandy and Beano comics that I picked up at a car boot sale several years ago. The game is called Scoop! In my relatively untouched 1988 version, the object of the game is that players compete for the front-page headlines with the help of an old red mock Bakelite telephone, blank 'newspaper' cards (*Today, News of the World, The Times* and the *Sun*), Scoop cards and a set of £100 cheques.

I recall an older version when I was still at school which I used to play with my best friend Cathy, and do not recall the rules being too brain taxing as a teenager, yet as I thumb through the instructions today it seems somewhat mind-boggling. It is all about which player gets to 'go to press' first in a race to get their news out there, whether it be sport or crime related, to do with advertising, involving a scandal or some other world exclusive, all striving towards a £2,500 bonus courtesy of the Fleet Street Cheque Bank.

I have to laugh at the irony. If I were to call my editor on the standard dial telephone now, would I get editorial permission to run the story that I have presented to you all today? Would he say 'yes', 'well done', call it a winner, scrap it or be permanently engaged, leaving me to mouth off in a series of exclamation marks amidst the F words as the 'story' goes? Would it fall under the category of a crime or a scandal or should I invent a 'crimandal'?

And as for the bonus thing, well he could keep the money towards my next lot of publishing fees if he thought for one minute my story worthy of a front page spread.

This wasn't the only game I found from the bygone days – I am also staring at my 1996 version of 'Headlines' in which players can work their way around the board by reading mickey take news on actual events that were happening at that time.

Fake news, the President of the United States would call it. Maybe he could revamp it in such a way as to suit his own end and have a bit of fun with Melania and the kids as the same time, if he could steal himself away from his Twitter page.

But joking aside and for anyone who has lost a loved one under similar circumstances I say to you, do not be fobbed off. You of all people will know that person better than anyone else. Do not feel intimidated by the white coats or the white ruffles on the navy blue uniforms. Challenge diagnoses – ensure differentials are explored – leave that place knowing you have done the best by those closest to you and then, and only then, will you feel able to sleep at night.

Don't go looking any further than your own backyard, because help that you may be promised is not actually out there in the first place, so all you can do is to get on with life the best you can, find solace in your family and become a writer.

I doubt I shall ever get to meet you in person, but if you happen to live near Kempton Park and like to put a bet or two on the gee-gees I have a tip for you. If you ever stumble across a horse called Clinical Negligence in the running, 'steer' well clear (pun intended) - it will be an odds on favourite that you will lose. Geppetto's boys (and girls) will continue to feast on scones and drink champagne from their wicker baskets as long as the public will allow them to sit in the woods and avoid the trees.

Like the business man who fought to get Bombay duck re-instated as a recognised dish, so too I have campaigned for over four years to be heard. I too went down the MP route and begged for the 'highest commissioner' in the coronial justice system to open a public enquiry into hubby's death, but I was not as successful.

It does little for one's ego that I take second place to a dried-up old fish – although I guess there are some similarities!

What was it that William Wallace once said? Oh yes, 'they took his life but they won't take his freedom of speech' *(Braveheart,* 1995).

Over time I have been made to feel like I am the one who is a sandwich short of their picnic and those in authority have banked on the fact that no matter how many letters I keep writing to all the different departments, sooner or later my ink well will run dry, but that will never happen, you see, because I have struck up this deal with my local officer suppliers to keep me in free ink in exchange for continuing to get my manuscripts bound by them so they can still keep their profits up!

So what would the Wicked Witch of the West have said as I dart between 1939 and 1995? Oh yes: 'I'll get you my pretties, and your little dogs too' *(Wizard of Oz,* 1939) and whilst I may adopt this motto as my own, the Wicked Witch of the West Country somehow sounds a bit naff by comparison don't you think?

Now there's just one more thing. Well, two actually. Firstly, I won first prize for my cake-baking skills back in the tent and secondly, next time you decide to cook liver and bacon, make sure the butcher has given you the right one or you might end up with pig or ox liver instead of lamb's. So liver is liver right, but again, trust me, they taste nothing like each other and it could be a recipe for disaster!

# EPILOGUE

—◦∞◦—

I would wager you thought that was the end of my story, but now that my mission to capture your attention has been accomplished, I intend to finish with a flourish that has the audience on its feet, like at the end of every 'Strictly Come Dancing' show.

Thank god that writing a book is not half as tricky as the prospect of having to master the American Smooth or the Fandango. Thank god my editor does not expect me to change into a different costume every time I write a new Halo, or dance cheek to cheek with him, 'butt' (pun intended) I bet his 'bottom' dollar he is keen to disassociate himself with anything that might seem remotely inappropriate, even if I am a wannabe film star.

There was strictly no couch casting during publication of my first novel and not once had anyone asked if they could 'check out my credentials' any more that I had sought to judge the designer by the book cover he has created for me, although I have to say it was rather nice. Nope! I need to brush aside any thoughts of a shimmery grey tie and a helicopter, especially as it might be a girl!

My mind is working overtime in another direction however. We have seen *Britain's Got Talent* and *The Voice*. But how about someone comes up with a TV series called *The Word*? There could be a panel, as usual, that consists of a literary agent, an editor, a publisher, and a graphic designer. It could work in the same way as *The Voice*, where the panel get only to hear narratives and the potential authors must disguise themselves in costumes that befit the story yet give nothing more away about them or their appearance, that their talent is based purely on what they have been able to create regardless of age, gender or otherwise.

But someone also needs to invent a new literary award. I have browsed some of the more coveted prizes, but I get my eyes checked at Vision Express, so the Specsavers National Book Awards are not for me. I drink tea and hate coffee, so the Costa book awards are a definite no-no.

Aiming for the one prestigious award that is left in the UK, the Nobel Prize is my one that got away since there can be no doubt that the love between Ted and me was requited and he did not have cholera (Gabriel

Garcia Marquez), which only leaves the Bailey's Woman's Prize, but for the fact that I am a Babycham girl.

So there's one for the would-be producers to work with – to invent a Babycham Book Award, bring back the Bambi and quite frankly my DEER and as Scarlett in my former altered ego state, I might just stand a chance! I have this great little green velvet number on standby.

Whilst the undertone of this story is that I have been 'Singing in the Rain' for so long now, it is time for me to 'Pick myself up, brush myself down and start all over again.' I need to find someone who can keep me in the lifestyle to which I had become accustomed.

I miss Ted, but I miss Bert too. Bert was our border collie, who I took to the Emerald City with me in my earlier fictitious time-travelling period. Apart from cocking his leg a few times on that yellow bricked pathway, he had been reasonably well behaved. He is still living on a farm in doggy heaven as far as Lola, our granddaughter, knows (*Emmerdale*, I think) but there is nothing stopping me from taking in another stray.

I shall go in search of my favourite TV collie, Lassie. Like me, she is probably getting on a bit, and we can keep each other company in my quiet house. Well, I say she, but rumour has it that whilst the furry mutt has always been portrayed on screen as a female, she is actually a 'he' – something to do with inconsistencies in the way they are groomed throughout the year that might leave the most observant of viewers confused. Never mind the audience, it is just as well that Lassie doesn't have to wear clothes, else there might be some concerns about he/she being a cross-breed cross dresser!

She always had this ability to make me cry when I used to watch her as a youngster, not least for her perseverance at trying to get reunited with her owner after she had gone off gallivanting, which always resulted in bleeding paws, extreme breathlessness and symptoms of hypothermia, having climbed every mountain and swum every ocean in a bid to get home. But if she were to try it with me she would have her own 'nursey- wursey' waiting back home to get out the bandages, the oxygen cylinder, the thermometer and warm blankets.

What made me cry even more, however, was the fact that she reportedly earned around £30,000 a year 'off screen' living in her own air-conditioned kennel and eating the biggest tins of Chum her money could buy, which is more than I can ever hope to rake in over the year in my job. Perhaps she could share it with me and I could exchange it for a *vacational* role. It is about time I had another holiday, so why shouldn't I get myself a sugar doggy daddy who will be quite content with me rubbing her ears and nothing more?

I can't swim, my fear of heights would prevent me from attempting any sort of mountain climbing and you have already established that I (OK, Dora) do not walk *anywhere*, so unless she finds *me* I shall have to consider Lassie to be a fictitious pet after all – the one who eventually leaves all her hard-earned cash to me in her will – in my dreams.

I have many a book to write, and this alone would adequately cover the fees to help me build up my own library of self-written material. If pets can express cupboard love, then why should the role not be reversed in humans?

I am wondering what the Littlest Hobo earns, or if he is even alive still – but he wouldn't let me adopt him anyway as he prefers to live on his own, so I have been told, so he would head off on his own at the end of each day in search of some other needy soul. Anyway, German shepherds can be a bit temperamental, can't they?

So a dog is a dog, but get the wrong one and it could end in disaster, just as a misdiagnosis and missed diagnosis resulted in them getting the wrong end of the doggy stick.

So desperate was I to be heard that I even contemplated taking my case to the European Court of Human Rights. Whilst the positive obligation under Article 2 requires the UK to take appropriate measures to protect patients' lives by compelling authorities to lay out certain regulations that seek to do just that, and whilst it also imposes upon the UK to make available an effective *independent* judicial system that will enable the cause of a patient's death in medical care to be determined and those held accountable, this is not what happens. Likewise the Article also subscribes to the punishment of any inadequate procedures that might infringe on a person's right to life where healthcare providers have not conformed to the legislative and administrative frameworks that seek to protect patients from such harm, but this does not happen either, and with only shirt-buttons to bargain with everything was nicely ironed out in favour of those who have the power.

As a teenager I remember my history teacher once asking me where the Magna Carta was signed and naively I said 'at the bottom.' I rest my case.

But perhaps I have been barking up the wrong tree all along and hubby and Bert are sending me a sign from above that I should try one more avenue. Perhaps it is a case for Scotland Yard. I have done a lot of the work for them already. I have managed to get the 'persons of interest' to commit their signatures to the attendance record. Their fingerprints are all over the 'swearing in' books and since no two fingerprints will be the same (or it is highly unlikely) then there is no need for a photofit or identi-parade. That will save time and money.

I am sure that with the evidence I already have by way of medical notes and drug charts and where there are gaps and missing pieces, the CID blokes will have the power to search through the Firchester's archives to retrieve the documents that I have been denied – on the premise that they were 'under no obligation to send them to me.' I am sure they would be able to spot any flaws in the paperwork and, given that the Firchester's recent government inspection has not passed it as being either safe, responsive or well-led with improvements required, surely this is enough basis upon which a warrant can be made to enter the premises, look into matters for me and hopefully initiate the investigation that I have so far been denied.

The best thing of all is that the police are renowned for opening up cases, no matter how long ago the 'crime' may or may not have been committed, so this could be my only hope, although I do not know if my arguments will be watertight.

So this is Brooke, signing out, going off duty, but not before paying credit to another Brooke bonding friend of mine, Shaw Taylor, who had taken time off from his police television programme (*Police 5,* from 1962 to 1992) to introduce me to a great new Police File card series from PG Tips during their heyday. However I was the one who had to do the detective work almost 40 decades ago by keeping my eyes open for cards I did not already have, which now makes up my complete pictorial collection of 40, so thanks Shaw for tipping me off as to the best way to go about getting them all.

Policing may have changed over the years, and so too nursing may have been given a revamp from the days of Florence Nightingale, but each job demands that the employee possesses the knowledge and skills needed to ensure a safe environment, whether it be in the wider community or within the confines of a healthcare setting, and failings should be treated on an equal footing for those who suffer as a result.

What do you call a clairvoyant midget who escaped from prison? Answer: A small medium at large.

What do you call a clinician working at a hospital

who escapes suggestions of medical negligence? Answer: Privileged.

So as Gobbie and Vinny pull the plugs on the pop-up courtroom, which deflates in a matter of seconds, the 'hearing' comes to a close. Gobbie asks me if I will allow him to take it home for his 'brother', who might be able to put it to good use should ITV go into lockdown for any reason.

'With pleasure,' I reply, thanking him for being so empathetic and entertaining at the same time.

Vinny is set to get the next plane out to Georgia – he realised he had left his toolkit in one of the plantation fields and he needs it for work next week when he is back fixing things that can be fixed.

The 'persons of interest' have gone their own way for now. The whole thing had been nothing short of a circus as the clowns were sent into the tent one by one to hear the account of someone who was far from laughing. But I know where to find them, because the circus is still in town.

As for me, I am off to the travel agents now to book two tickets to Venezuela. Intrigued as to what happens next? Join me next time and I will tell you.

Thanks for listening!

www.ingramcontent.com/pod-product-compliance
Lightning Source LLC
Chambersburg PA
CBHW072125170626
46813CB00004B/1696